p. 5. No! p. 44

p. 69

p. 74 sure p...

p. 112 ?

p. 146, 147?

p. 151 — south, driving

p. 120 what judgment do if — qu. reg
                              here ?

Kristin and Boone

Kristin and Boone

KAREN ROSE AND LYNDA HALFYARD

Oct. 27, 83

For Eleanor,
Still, after so many
years, my "ideal"
writer. Much love,
Karen

Dear Eleanor — Have
been borrowing your
books from Karen & loving
Them! Best Wishes

Houghton Mifflin Company Boston 1983

Lynda Halfyard

Library of Congress Cataloging in Publication Data

Rose, Karen.
  Kristin and Boone.

  Summary: A young, talented and selfish actress
discovers some important values through her friendship
with a brilliant director who happens to be a dwarf.
  [1. Actors and actresses—Fiction. 2. Dwarfs—Fiction.
3. Friendship—Fiction. 4. Television—Fiction]
I. Halfyard, Lynda.   II. Title.
PZ7.R717Kr 1983   [Fic]   83-12580
ISBN 0-395-34560-X

Printed in the United States of America

P 10 9 8 7 6 5 4 3 2 1

For MICHAEL DUNN
1934–1973

— K.R.

For my father
and in loving memory
of my mother

— L.H.

CONTENTS

Kristin and
Boone

[1] Scanning the Universe for Likely People

STUDIO MONITOR SHOWS:
[Control Room: Shining levers and buttons and switches and lights that glow and pulse. Above are many small screens set edge to edge. In front a dark form crouches, watching the screens, each with a different, changing picture: people, cities, wilderness, mountains, rivers, jungles. The shape moves, following the images. Stops. A hand moves toward the panel — a terrible hand, large and gray and twisted — and all the screens but one blink out.]
[On that screen a beautiful young girl smiles. The picture grows, filling all the screens. The girl is surrounded by others: a man, a boy, a girl. The hand moves again to the panel and the girl's face fills the screen. In profile, the monstrous head of a beast is silhouetted against the glowing young face.]
[He smiles. He has found what he was looking for.]

"Speed," the assistant director said, and I heard the whine of the sound machine.

"Marker!" The clapboard, reading "ONCE UPON A GALAXY: SCENE 1, TAKE 4," snapped shut.

[Beauty, her father, brother and sister, stand

1

before a ruined spaceship. The land beyond is brooding, barren desert.]

I stepped onto the masking tape indicating my camera position on the set.

"Action!" Boone called.

I spoke my first lines.

Beauty: Father, you mustn't blame yourself.

Father: Who else should I blame? We're here on this barren planet with no hope of escape. With no hope.

Brother: I want to go home, Father.

Sister: *[Starts to cry.]* So do I.

Beauty: *[Crossing to comfort her.]* Later we'll tell stories. Would you like that?

Father: Stories! This is no story, Beauty. This is real. We've just the supplies from the ship. And then?

Beauty: *[Draws the children to her and looks over them to her father.]* I know, Father.

"Cut! *Cut!* CUT!" Boone bounced off his chair and came toward us in the sudden silence. We all turned to watch him, waiting for his new pronouncement. I was sure it was for me. It was.

"Kristin. This is *not* an intergalactic beauty pageant."

I flushed and my lips tightened.

Boone went on in his deep, resonant voice. "You can't just look beautiful and helpless. *Our* Beauty is brave. Resolute. Curious. *A warrior!*"

"A warrior?" I kept the skepticism from my voice.

"*A warrior!*" he repeated. "Think of it this way: They are in an absolutely hopeless situation. They are going to starve to death. But Beauty isn't crying. She's making the best of things. Her father thinks she doesn't understand. But she *does*. She knows the terrible truth and she is MAKING THE BEST OF IT!"

Boone talks like that, in capitals and italics. It does get him the undivided attention of the actors.

"I see," I said.

"Do you see, Kristin? Then let *us* see." He walked away from us with that springing waddle that is, I had decided, worse from the back. He got into his special director's chair with a clever hop and mid-air twist. He was terribly agile, given his shape.

We did the whole thing again — this was not the first time — and when we came to the disputed line, I found, from someplace in the depths of my head, the image of a pioneer woman facing the unknown. I pulled my younger brother and sister to me and looked at my father and knew that he, too, was going to die here on this blasted planet.

Beauty: *[Draws the children to her and looks over them to her father.]* I know, Father.

"*Cut! Print take four!*" From his chair he nodded at me. "You *did* see, Kristin."

That was about the level of appreciation I

3

usually got from Boone. It was not — or *not,* as Boone would say — what I was used to getting. "Thank you, Mr. Boone." I smiled.

[Control Room: The Beast watches the sad group. His hands move toward the dials, the ugly fingers twisting delicately. On the screen Beauty's eyes widen as she looks over her father's shoulder to the desert beyond. There is a shimmer in the cold desert air, a shimmer that gathers body and depth and definition as she watches.]

Beauty: Father! Look!!

[They all turn toward the desert.]

Father: A ship! But where . . . *[Breaks off.]*

[In the near distance a silver spaceship glitters in the cold sun of the planet.]

Beauty: It just . . . appeared.

"Cut! *Cut!*" Again Boone came toward us. "I know it's hard," he said, even before he was close, "since you can't *see* it. But you'll have to use whatever imagination you can muster. There is a spaceship out there. And there wasn't a minute ago. You," he nodded at my father, "are shocked, but at the same time hopeful, grateful, awed, terrified. Not just a little surprised."

I listened carefully, knowing my turn would come.

"And you, Kristin. Somewhere in the depths of another studio, a handful of terribly talented men are working to create a shimmering, materializing spaceship. With any luck at all, millions of people will see that spaceship appear before

4

their eyes. They will be awed by the magic of special effects."

I nodded. We'd heard this before about the wizards, the men who worked with lights and film and models to make pictures like ours possible.

"But for now, since we don't *have* a materializing spaceship right here, we need some special effects from *you*. On screen, when the ship appears, the audience is going to have to believe that you saw it appear. Shall we try it again?"

So we did. And again and again. Until Boone was finally satisfied with the expressions on my face. I'm sure he was convinced he had inspired us all, but personally the only expression that I was conscious of having on my face was confusion.

We broke for lunch, just in time for me to get to an interview. As I was leaving, Boone appeared next to me. I looked down at him and then away. I refused to slow my walk, knowing that he had to scurry to keep pace with me. After all, he had chosen to walk with me.

"You did that very well, Kristin."

I stopped in surprise and turned, but he was already leaving, head high, little legs working. I shrugged and went to meet the reporter from *TV World*.

WINTER: How, then, did you start your career?
KRISTIN: Innocently, with no preplanning, if

you'd believe it. Phyllis Star is my mother's friend, you know. One day we just happened to be at her office. As you know, she books both theatrical and commercial stuff, and a call came in for kids who were overweight, could jog and make it for a four o'clock call that afternoon.

WINTER: Surely you weren't overweight.

KRISTIN: Slightly, but I was just slightly enough for my mom's friend to say to me, "Kristin, you want to go try out for a commercial?"

I told her, "I can't open my mouth, Phyllis. What if they ask me to say something?"

She said, "You just opened your mouth."

And so I went. It was a big office in a bank building, just plain, a waiting room like a dentist's, and I sat down with thirty-five other overweight and slightly overweight girls my age and older. Sign your name, somebody said, and I did. One by one they went in and they came out. What would I do, I thought, if I had to say something?

A girl came by and I asked her, "What did you have to say?"

She said, "Nothing. Just jog." And she walked on out.

My turn came. I went in and bright lights flashed at me. A voice somewhere behind a light said, "Pick up the book on that table and turn toward the camera, turn a page and look bored." So I did that.

He said, "Do it again." Then he said, "Okay. Jog in place until we tell you to stop."

I jogged a bit, they said stop and then said, "How do you feel?"

I said, "Fine," and they said, "She talks, too. Thank you for your time, good-bye now." And out I went.

WINTER: Well, I never saw that commercial, but it is hard to believe that you got your start that way.

KRISTIN: It won an award-of-the-year for Knudsen. I jogged, drank the milk, said, "Something worth running for," and got a commercial award.

WINTER: Is that when you first knew that you wanted to act?

KRISTIN: Oh, no. I always knew I didn't want to act.

WINTER: Well, Kristin, we are indeed lucky for that milk commercial, aren't we?

KRISTIN: Yes, we are.

WINTER: Is acting easy for you now?

KRISTIN: It really is. It has become something I try to take in stride, a regular part of my life.

WINTER: How did you get this part?

KRISTIN: Mr. Boone saw me in *Not Alone at Sea*.

WINTER: People are spreading rumors about your possibly getting an Emmy nomination. I'll certainly be back if you do. Okay?

KRISTIN: Of course.

WINTER: Perfect. Thank you. See you in *TV World*.

KRISTIN: Thank you.

Walking toward my dressing room, I passed Maggie Arnold, the set teacher and social worker. Last winter I worked with a lady I was crazy about, but Maggie Arnold does not inspire me. She's a hoverer and, while always present, never contributes anything of value. As I passed her now, she said, "Good interview, Kristin."

"Thanks." She was nice enough, just no inspiration. Fortunately, in the summer I wasn't required to do a specific number of hours of schoolwork per day on the set, so her job came down to making sure Boone gave us an hour for lunch, which he always did.

I went into my dressing room, sat down in front of my mirror and realized that I was alone for the first time since five that morning. I looked up at the mirror and gave myself a beautiful smile, the one that got the milk-commercial award, in fact. So, people were speaking about my getting an Emmy nomination.

Taking off my make-up, I mentally made notes on the interview and on what I had said. There was the chance that I'd be doing quite a few interviews in the weeks to come, and I didn't want obvious inconsistencies if I could help it, although I had been told by other actors and actresses that what you said in an interview didn't have to be truthful or even consistent as long as it was interesting. Lying to reporters had come easily to me. The truth was a long-gone thing in my life.

What truth, I wondered, had I left out of this one, and what lie put in? Two lies put in, one truth left out, or was it just plain three lies, to be honest about it?

The biggest lie, but who will ever know: "I always knew I didn't want to act."

There has never been anything I have wanted to be but a brilliant, popular and successful actress. When my teachers took a part away from me in fifth grade, simply because I was taller than the boy who played my father, I knew that someday they'd be aware of their error. I thought that it might take longer than perhaps it is going to take if I am lucky this week. I have already learned that show business is a lot of being in the right place at the right time. We'll see.

I doubt that my next lie will ever be uncovered, unless I become really famous, internationally famous, and then, in old age, tell all.

"Is acting easy for you now?"

"It really is. It has become something I try to take in stride, a regular part of my life."

And the truth of that is that there is this fear that comes over me every time I step before the camera — actually, even when I am in my dressing room, even if I am not alone, even when they

9

are putting make-up on me, even right as they are doing it. I can be saying to the girl, "Just don't make me look so much like Dracula," and I laugh and she laughs and inside me the fear is spreading out. It is as much physical as mental. It goes through my belly into my thighs. It is in my throat and in my brain. In my head it makes a noise that is so loud I am always surprised that people, even I, can go on talking and being heard above it.

But today's other lie — that may have been a mistake. From what I have heard about Adam Michael Boone, he doesn't pay much attention to the press, if any at all, so perhaps he won't find out what I said, or if he does perhaps he won't feel it necessary to tell them how I actually got the part. As far as I know, he has never seen *Not Alone at Sea*. And he hardly came after me.

My agent, Clive Wheat, called me a few months ago.

FLASHBACK
"Listen, Kristin, there's a part I want you to read for. It's a starring role in a movie. Are you listening?"

"Yes, breathlessly, Clive. Go on."

He laughed. "Well, it's for the role of Beauty — "

"You've got to be kidding," I interrupted.

"Be quiet and listen. It's a modern *Beauty and the Beast* and it's called *Once upon a Galaxy*."
10

"I don't want to be in a children's thing," I said.

"Well, I want you to. If — and I am only saying *if*, remember that — you were to get an Emmy nomination for playing a sixteen-year-old in the world of adult men, it would be very good publicity for you to be then working in a movie for children, in the role of a sixteen- or seventeen-year-old."

My agent knows the business.

"Okay," I said. "Who's doing it?"

"Adam Michael Boone's directing, is all I know for sure. The Beast's not cast yet, though most of the other roles are."

"Is Adam Michael Boone that dwarf?"

"It's not nice to talk like that, Kristin. In answer to your question, yes."

"And he wants me?"

"Well, that's the thing, Kristin. Not exactly."

"Clive, exactly what does 'not exactly' mean? Why are we having this conversation?"

"Okay, here it is. I sent your name in with the breakdowns and didn't get a callback. I called Betty Fisher, who's doing the casting and is my wife's friend, and she said they had considered you carefully, for your looks were perfect, they thought, but didn't call you in because Boone felt you were too young for Beauty."

"Okay, so I didn't get it. Why are you keeping me from my homework?"

"I got you a chance to read for it. I'm not

11

known as the greatest agent in the world for no reason, you know."

"Your wife talked to Betty Fisher, etcetera, right?"

"Right."

"When do I read?"

"Tomorrow afternoon. Either I or Dewey will pick you up after school and take you over to Boone's."

"No script to look at tonight?"

"He wants a cold reading. You could always reread *Beauty and the Beast*. Frankly, honey, I think you'll get it. You may not be old, but you're more beautiful than anyone they are considering and Boone will see that. He will also see that you look sixteen. Just be sure to look sixteen tomorrow, okay?"

"Okay."

I did reread *Beauty and the Beast*. It certainly was wholesome.

Clive himself met me after school the next afternoon, so I knew he wanted badly for me to have the role. Probably very good money. Money he discussed with my mother, and she was very good at that, having dealt with such issues in her own work.

Boone was holding the readings in his office on the Twentieth Century lot. There were six Beautys in the outer office. I felt they were all at least as pretty as I am, and they were certainly older.

One by one they went in, called in by Betty Fisher herself. One by one they came out and I was finally beckoned in.

It was a big office and there were quite a few people in it. I was directed to a desk at the front of the office.

"Kristin Kelley, right?" a deep, vital voice asked.

"Right," I said, and saw Adam Michael Boone for the first time. It flashed through my head that maybe he judged who would get the part on her reaction to him. I tried for nonchalance, a desperate try — for Adam Michael Boone is not someone you easily take in with a glance, smiling an introduction in his direction.

Of course I expected him to be small. And he was. I was more than a head taller.

He came toward me. His walk was awkward but certain. From his little feet up, he was very, very small. Then, suddenly, there was a flash of what might be a normal body, and then his head. In the few seconds it took him to reach me, I understood that all of Adam Michael Boone was in that head. It was not unhandsome. His features were clear, his eyes were crystal blue, his lips were parted in a welcome grin, and he had full, brown, wavy hair with touches of gray.

He handed me the script. "I must tell you, Miss Kelley, that I am listening to you read only because Miss Fisher has been insistent on your behalf. I have no doubt that you are a capable actress, but I have been looking for someone older."

"I understand," I said

Now he looked at me. Very carefully. "You are very beautiful," he said, and walked slowly to the back of the room, where he sat among the others who were watching.

"Read the marked sections," he said. "Take a minute to look them over."

I opened the script.

It was the part where Beauty decided to keep her word to the Beast to go back to him. I read it over.

"I'm ready," I said.

Boone said, "I will read the father's lines."

Father: What is the matter?

Beauty: I must return to the Beast.

Father: But why?

Beauty: I only know that something is calling me to him. If I do not go back, he will die of grief.

Father: What should that be to you?

Beauty: I don't know, but it is something.

Boone said, "Let's do it again."

We did it again. This time I put a slow, lingering emphasis on the last word, "something." So that it would be clear to all that this *something* had become a magnet powerful beyond anything.

"Thank you, Miss Kelley. That will be all. When we make a decision in a day or so, your agent will get a callback if we want you."

I could tell I didn't get it. No one had ever heard me read so little for a part. He'd just been courteous to his casting director. I was too young, and although he had said I was beautiful, next to the other girls I felt merely pretty.

Well, it had been something to meet Boone, anyway. He was quite a sight. No wonder his reputation as an actor had been so great. He could grab any audience anywhere just by stepping center stage. He wouldn't have to be much of an actor, either. And sympathy, no doubt. A lot of sympathy from the audience. I had never seen him act.

How he had become a director was unclear to me. But here, too, his reputation was excellent. I had recently seen one of the movies he directed — a perfectly paced, lighthearted comedy about a married couple in New York who raised geckos to sell to people with cockroach problems. It was funny and Boone did get some extraordinary acting out of the geckos.

And now he had a chance to get some extraordinary acting out of me, but I left the office reasonably certain there'd be no callback.

But there was. He was definitely considering me for the role and wanted me to read again, with one other actress. She and I faced each other in that outer office one morning, and then she got called in. "Good luck," I lied.

After about fifteen minutes she came out, walked by me and left the office.

Another five minutes and I was called in.

Same setup.

He had me read the same lines again, this time opposite John Sylvester, who was to play the part of the father.

Then he said, "Try the line, 'If I do not go back, he will die of grief,' again, and say it sadly. You have to make a choice you wish you didn't have to make."

I read it again.

"That is awful, Miss Kelley."

"I'm sorry," I said. He was the first director ever to say such a thing to me. What made him such an expert on Beauty's lines? Beast's, maybe. I expected him to dismiss me rapidly.

"Miss Kelley, why do you want this role in a production designed for children when, I understand, you have played a role in a major prime-time movie with an adult audience in mind?"

"Did you see it?" I asked. The way he stood there, small and smug, taunted me, and I didn't like him.

"No," he said. "But I did catch one of your milk commercials. Very good." He laughed.

The others in the room laughed too. They could buy his jokes at my expense.

"But you haven't answered my question: Why do you want this role?"

"To work with one of the biggest directors in town," I said, and I said the line to leave no doubt that I had carefully chosen the word "big-

16

gest.'' After all, I wasn't going to get the part anyway.

There was the start of laughter but its abrupt cessation.

"Flattery, Miss Kelley, will get you nowhere.''

"May I go?" I asked.

"No," he said and laughed. "Read the line again. Treat the word 'grief' with proper respect.''

I took a deep breath and read it again.

"That's much better," he said. "You'll hear from us.''

And I did.

END FLASHBACK

I still didn't like him. At the audition I was "terrible" and today — what was it? "This is *not* an intergalactic beauty pageant." Thinking about it made me so angry that I took out my dart set, wrote his name on the dartboard and threw darts at it until I felt silly and ready to go home.

Dewey, Clive's gofer and sort of my personal chauffeur, was waiting to take me home.

"Did you see the Beast yet?" he asked.

"Yes, today.''

"Is it good?"

"Gruesome," I said. Dewey was an avid science fiction buff.

"Who's playing it?"

"Keith Winslow."

"I saw him in an episode of *Little House on the Prairie*. What's he like?"

"I don't know what he's like," I said, "but a beast he ain't."

Dewey laughed and said, "Watch out. Leading ladies shouldn't fall in love with leading beasts."

It was still early in the afternoon, so he asked me if I wanted to be dropped off at some friend's house. I mumbled that I had stuff to do at home. There really was no place to drop me off. No one's. I have never had the knack of making friends. I never seemed to be in the same places they were. Perhaps it is my work. But also perhaps it is something in me. It doesn't matter, though. I wouldn't have it any other way. I don't understand people who aren't after something, whose only goals are a soda after school, some homework, telephone calls and TV. They never seem to be going anywhere. They do not go to sleep every night, as I do, praying that they will get an Emmy nomination.

CLAPBOARD: ONCE UPON A GALAXY, SCENE 6

[In front of the ruined spaceship: The younger children are playing with shiny new toys. Beauty is watching her father.]

Beauty: Why can't we all go?

Father: I must see where this ship will take us.

Beauty: Father, don't go. There was enough food in the spaceship to last a long time.

Father: Beauty, my dear, I have to go. This is our only hope.

Beauty: *[Shivering, hugging herself.]* We're together here. If you don't come back . . .

Father: I will. Somehow I know I will.

Brother: When are you going, Father?

Father: Soon.

Sister: Bring me a ring. Bring me lots of shiny rings.

Beauty: Oh, little sister. Don't — *[Breaks off.]*

Father: *[Gently.]* They're so used to my bringing back presents. Let them hope, Beauty.

Beauty: Of course.

Brother: I want a Mark XII rocket horse.

Sister: I want a new dress.

Father: I'll try. *[Hugs them.]* And you, Beauty? What can I bring for you?

Beauty: Come back to us, Father. That is all I ask.

Father: Ask me for something, Beauty. I want you to.

Beauty: *[Looks longingly at the stark land, the tumbled rocks that are all that can be seen in every direction.]* If it's summer where you are, bring me a rose.

"Cut! *Cut!* CUT!"

I froze, the way I always did when Boone shouted at us. What could be wrong? I thought I had done that very well, and the cameras had been on me, so the fact that I had seen Margo, my "little sister," scratching her nose could not have made him interrupt me.

He hopped down from his chair and came

19

toward us with that springing waddle. "That was very nice, Kristin," he said. He always said that, looking up at you from his big eyes. "I want you to do it again."

I groaned.

He ignored me. "Do it again, saying 'If it's summer where you go, bring me a rose.' And as you say 'bring me a rose,' turn from the window and look at your father." He turned away, satisfied with himself, I guess.

Beauty: If it's summer where you go *[turns from window and looks at father]*, bring me a rose.

"Cut! *Cut!*"

I couldn't believe it. I thought it had been perfect, but there was Boone, hopping down again, hopping toward us again.

"That's better, Kristin."

"Thank you." I was always polite to him. Even when it was very difficult, as it was right now.

"When you look out, Kristin, all you see is desert."

I knew that. I didn't actually see it, of course. There was nothing where I looked. The desert would appear later, thanks to the film editors and the special-effects people. And Boone knew that I knew it. After all, he had taken half an hour yesterday to explain it to everyone.

Boone went on as if he were talking to himself: "Desert. Nothing but rocks and sand. Cold. Couldn't be less like summer." He hit himself on

the forehead with the palm of his hand. I thought
it was an affected gesture, but he did it so often
that I had almost learned to ignore it. "That's
it," he said, bouncing on his little legs. "You're
to say 'If it's summer *anywhere*,' turn from the
window and let us see the loss of summer on
your face, then 'bring me a rose.' All right,
everybody, let's do it again."

He looked delighted with himself. How much
difference could a word make, I wondered, but
obediently, like a good little child actress, I went
back to my place by the window. I looked out
and saw the desert. I could hear Boone's voice in
my head: "The loss of summer."

Beauty: If it's summer anywhere *[turns from win-
dow],* bring me a rose.

"Cut!" Boone came forward again. "Think
about 'anywhere,' Kristin. Anywhere is very big,
isn't it?"

"Yes."

"She's not asking him to look on the Twentieth Century lot, is she?"

"No."

"How big *is* it, Kristin?"

"The Twentieth Century lot?"

"The universe. Isn't that what 'anywhere' is?"

"Trillions of light-years."

"At least," he said. "How many roses do you
suppose there are?"

"Well," I said, "if I knew how many flower
shops there are — "

21

"Stop joking," Boone said.

"I don't know how many roses there are in the universe."

"The universe is a vast array of secrets. Everything about the universe is still secret. It is very big, trillions upon trillions of light-years big. Yes?"

"Yes," I said.

"And amongst those light-years it is definitely a secret as to how many planets spin around how many suns, isn't it?"

"Yes."

"It is a secret how many of those planets have life. Yes?"

"Yes."

"Then before you say your line, think of the enormous secret it is as to how many of those life-supporting planets grow roses."

The crew laughed. I didn't. If there was anything I hated, it was humiliation. Never before had a director treated me this way.

We did it again.

Beauty: If it's summer anywhere *[turns from window]*, bring me a rose.

"*Cut!* CUT! Print take seven! *Beautiful!* BEAUTIFUL!" Boone hopped down again, looking more than ever like a windup toy, the way he did when he was excited about something — waving his little arms, tipping his big head back to look up at us all. "Perfect. You were great, everybody. See you after lunch." And he was gone.

I wouldn't have admitted it to Boone, but that last time it *felt* right. I don't know if it was my feeling of humiliation or the new word or Boone's talking about the enormity of the universe, but when I said the line again, I felt tears in my eyes.

Which isn't a bad thing. Tears make my eyes look bluer and bigger. They shine for the cameras.

I gave a Boone-like jiggle as I walked away. Very subdued. Anyone would believe it was just girlish high spirits.

We had one more scene to do that day, or at least one that I was in. The hostile planet we saw beyond our ruined spaceship wasn't there. Some other time, on location, Beauty's father would walk bravely over the rocky landscape to the silver ship that would take him searching for help. Today the rest of us, little brother and sister and I, had to watch him leave. That doesn't sound hard, but Boone didn't like the way we watched.

"My God!" he shouted. "You look like your father's gone to the corner market." Actually he yelled at all of us, but I knew he was talking to me. After all, even Boone wouldn't yell at those children.

"Do you *know* where he's going? Do you KNOW? He's going into . . . space." His voice dropped on the word "space" and suddenly I saw . . . space. A blackness. A vast emptiness.

"Space. That is where your father is going. Strapped unconscious in his chair, he will tumble with the ship. Suddenly" — and Boone lifted his hand to us — "there is silence. The ship stops tumbling. Your father is still, his head bent forward. The ship floats aimlessly into the blackness of space until it is a silver needle among the star dots and is gone."

I had been wrong. Boone was an actor.

We did it again. The children stared, which seemed to be all they could do, and that seemed to satisfy Boone. They still looked stunned from his monologue. I was, too, but I apparently didn't look stunned enough. I watched and watched and watched. Humbly, hopefully, sadly, bravely, fearfully. With a hint of tears. Without. Head held high, head bowed. I think what he had in mind was all of them simultaneously. When a director tells you what he wants you to do, the possibility that it's something that nobody could ever do seems not to occur to him. At least it didn't to Boone. Probably, I thought, he could do it, this mysterious way of looking that he wanted from me.

We went on and on. And Boone's voice began to level out.

Apparently I was getting closer. Already I had learned, or thought that I had learned, that as the scene began to approach the idea he had of it, he used fewer and fewer italics and capitals.

I could tell that something was happening on the set that had nothing to do with the scene. It was not from any noise, for shooting was still going on, but when the cameras and attention were not on me — and they were often on my father in the scene — I could look out and see new shadows slipping around behind the crew. I was tired anyway and happy when Boone called, "Cut! Print take ten, save six and eight."

The first person I saw was my agent, Clive Wheat, pushing his big, sloppy, energetic body forward. Behind him it looked like half the cast and crew were gathered, and I thought I also saw the man who had interviewed me a few days ago.

Wheat was exuberant. "You've got it, baby. The Emmy nomination!"

The Emmy nomination. A surge of pleasure began in me, and I wanted to know if any of the others — I had been the only girl in the cast — had gotten nominations. I opened my mouth to speak, but Wheat had me by the arm.

"Over here, baby. They all want you over here."

He hushed everybody into silence, which embarrassed me, but I reminded myself that I had worked very hard to get this agent. Clive Wheat was known to take what he had and do a lot with it. Jovial, flip and pleasant right to the edge of the bargaining table, where he became as tough as necessary.

"Ladies and gentlemen of *Once upon a Galaxy*, may I present to you your star and future Emmy winner for her outstanding performance in *Not Alone at Sea*."

A few people clapped and I heard a few cheers. Boone came up to me and said, "Congratulations, Kristin. I also hope you know your lines for tomorrow's shooting."

Wheat reached out to take Boone's arm, but I saw him flinch before he touched Boone. He dropped his arm to his side. "Boone, you've got yourself a star, miles of free publicity, and has she ever not known her lines? Give her a break."

"She's not a star. I don't have stars on my sets. I don't need miles of any kind of publicity. She muffed three lines this very afternoon, and what kind of break did you have in mind? Champagne for the entire crew?"

Boone must be jealous, I decided. I would try to play it his way. "It's a nomination, Clive. Just a nomination."

But Clive Wheat knew me well already. He pulled me to the side. "Oh, come on, kid, this is your Uncle Wheat over here. Is it just any old nomination, like to homeroom secretary, maybe?"

"Oh, I'm glad, but — "

"But, baloney. I've got to go. Dewey will drive you home later. *TV World* is here for an interview. Be good and be sure to mention that the cameraman was nominated too.''

And he was gone.

I could tell immediately that this was very unlike the first interview, when only Maggie Arnold had bothered to listen. This time it got quiet and I had the sensation that everybody was listening to me. This is a very special sensation to me. I have a sense of intensity that almost lifts me off the ground. It's what I think taking bows will be like when I act on the stage someday. It makes me feel that everything I'm saying is special, rare and true.

WINTER: Hi, there. Didn't know we'd be speaking so soon. Congratulations, Kristin. I hope you have time to talk.

KRISTIN: Yes. I'd be happy to.

WINTER: How does it feel to have been nominated for an Emmy in your very first big production?

KRISTIN: Well, Mr. Winter —

WINTER: Please, call me Larry, if you will.

KRISTIN: Well, Larry, it feels good. It's just luck, of course. Having been in the right place at the right time.

WINTER: Modesty is always becoming, Kristin, and obviously you have it. But we'd like to get at the inside story of your emotions. How does it feel to be picked over all your

27

colleagues? Not one of them got a nomination, if you notice.

KRISTIN: I do believe I got it because I was the only girl on shipboard with all those men. It certainly gave me a chance to stand out in the crew. And you evidently didn't notice, but Burt Evans, the cameraman of *Not Alone at Sea,* is up for an Emmy. He's the one who deserves it, much more so than I do.

WINTER: Modesty again, Kristin. Do you think you'll get the Emmy?

KRISTIN: It's not something I would allow myself to think about, Larry. I don't believe it's something an actress should deal with. I have a serious role right now in Mr. Boone's production and that is where my energy is going. Do you understand what I mean?

WINTER: Oh, yes, yes, of course. You're Beauty, I understand, in this new tale of outer space.

KRISTIN: Yes, I am.

WINTER: It's certainly very obvious why you would get such a role, Kristin. But what made you want to go from an adult movie to a story designed for children? It is, after all, a fancy remake of *Beauty and the Beast,* isn't it?

KRISTIN: Well, let me answer that in several ways: The main reason for taking the role is for the opportunity to work with Adam Michael Boone. Any actress would grab at that, I think, don't you?

WINTER: Well, yes, that would be a motivating factor. And what other reasons?

KRISTIN: Well, you know, there's nothing wrong with children. It sounds as though you assume that acting for young people is somehow less important than acting for an adult audience.

WINTER: I don't mean to imply that.

KRISTIN: Your question does imply that, though. I feel that every performance an actress gives — whether to children, adults, a small audience, a large audience, a TV camera or a Broadway theatergoer — every performance should be a summation of all the skills she has developed thus far in her career.

WINTER: Well, I certainly can't disagree with that. Why, do you suppose, did Mr. Boone decide to do a rewrite of a fairy tale?

KRISTIN: You'd have to ask him that.

WINTER: *(clearing his throat)* Yes, well, I do hope to interview him someday. Why do you, Kristin, feel this story is worth doing again?

(It had not been something I had thought about at all. After all, had it been *Hansel and Gretel* I would have taken the role. It flipped through my mind that the director would be great doing *Snow White and the Seven,* but I managed not to say that one out loud. It would be exactly the sort of thing that could ruin one in print.)

KRISTIN: This particular story is worth doing again at this particular time, I think, because in a time when women's rights are expanding

29

and women are becoming more independent every day — and of course this is rightfully so because we have been a put-down group — I think that in such a time it is also important for children to realize that romance is also still important. That it is still important for a girl to want to find her prince and that the prince must still find his special woman. It is not really that Beauty is beautiful that is important, but that she is the special choice of the prince. It is —

WINTER: *(interrupting)* I see clearly now, Kristin, why you have chosen this as your next role, and we will all be waiting to see it on the screen. I think it likely that any prince would choose you for his Beauty.

(I tried to blush. I think it would be the most appropriate response to comments about my appearance, but I can't do it too well yet. It's unpredictable. I think "blush" to myself, and sometimes it works and sometimes not. I have had absolutely nothing to do with the way I look, and when praised for this part of me, I am really partly displeased and partly just not clear how to respond. "Thank you" seems silly, "Oh, I'm not that beautiful" sounds conceited and "I had nothing to do with my looks" seems a put-down to the person who really probably thinks he's saying something sweet to me, something that will make me feel good. Blushing, I think, is the answer. If only I can get it down pat before too

30

much more time passes. I am as little overjoyed by comments on my beauty as I would be if someone told me I dried dishes well. Some things are irrelevant to one's ego. I like to be told I'm bright. And good at my work.

I think the blush came off this time, because he smiled warmly at me as I answered him.)

KRISTIN: I do hope you'll enjoy the film.

WINTER: Certainly I will. Well, remember your friend Larry. I'd like an exclusive with you in the event — probability, if you want my opinion — that you do win that Emmy in six weeks' time. Will you think of me then, Kristin?

KRISTIN: *Then* is such a long way off. I've a film to shoot. I won't be thinking about the Emmys very much. Boone doesn't have it on our shooting schedule.

I watched Larry walk off the set, jotting as he went, turning me into print, half of which would appear in *TV World* and half of which would be crumpled up and thrown away.

The people who had been standing around listening to the interview drifted off, and I was free to go to my dressing room. As I crossed the set I noticed Boone standing at the coffee table with a cup of coffee in his hand. He looked directly at me, his head tilted up, and I could not miss the expression of disdain in his eyes. I should have kept on walking. "Why are you looking at me like that?" I asked instead.

"Like what?" he replied, sipping his coffee.

"It's the look on your face when someone blows a line."

He laughed.

"Now why are you laughing?"

"Sometimes I think I should have gotten a child for this role."

"What do you mean by that?"

He hesitated, and I thought he was about to say "Nothing," the way my mother often will after she has said something provocative like that. I can never get the next words out of her. It is a torture adults do to children that other children never do more than once, because they get beat up for it.

"Well, since I said that much," he went on, at least showing enough sensitivity not to leave me hanging, "I guess I should go on."

"Do," I said, with a sarcastic tone that might be a little dangerous with one's director.

"You're slick, as if you have been acting for a century or so. I can't help thinking that if you're like this now, what will you be like at twenty-one?"

"When was I slick? What scene?"

He shrugged his shoulders. "That's the mystery of it. Not in the scenes. I couldn't bear that. You wouldn't be here."

"Where? In the interview?"

"Yes."

"Who told you to listen?"

"If I could have avoided listening, I would have. When everybody else listens and there is nobody for me to talk to or work with, I listen."

"An interview is only an interview."

"That's what I mean, you're slick."

"Do you think it's a bad image for Beauty? Is that what you're driving at?"

"I'm not all that big on images, Kristin. I don't even believe in them. I just don't think your attitude is all that good for you."

No one talks to me that way. "I really don't think this is any of your business," I said. "Only my mother has the right to talk to me that way."

He shook his head. "Okay." He turned away, but then turned back. "While we're on the subject, you don't understand the script."

"*Once upon a Galaxy*?"

"You don't even understand *Beauty and the Beast,* the fairy tale."

I felt a need to defend myself. "I was only talking from the top of my head," I said.

"From the top of your head, you've got it all wrong."

"How?"

"Don't worry," he said. "If your feminist interpretation gets into your performance, I'll explain it to you line by line."

His tone of voice was so superior that if I hadn't been so much bigger than he was, I'd have hit him, I think. I did not respond.

"You really want to win that Emmy, don't you?"

"What business is that of yours, Mr. Boone?"

He put his coffee cup down. "You're absolutely right, Kristin. It's none of my business. Nor was your interview. Forgive me." And he walked away from me.

Forgive him, my foot. He's small, but hugely arrogant. As I walked to the dressing room, Maggie Arnold stopped me.

"Congratulations, Kristin. Pay no attention to Mr. Boone. I liked your interpretation. It will be good for women's rights."

Somehow Maggie Arnold's liking my interpretation didn't cheer me at all. I went into my dressing room vaguely dissatisfied with myself.

Printed in greasepaint across the mirror was "GOOD LUCK FROM BEAST KEITH." He probably meant it, I thought.

Boone was right about one thing — that I had lines to study — so I picked up the script to begin working on the next day's lines. Dewey was due in a few minutes, but just now there was not a sound around me and the quietness settled in. I packed up my stuff and left my dressing room. The set was dark, everything waiting, about to be used to make magic. It was awesome in a way that I loved, yet empty in a way that almost frightened me. What was I doing alone when I'd just received an Emmy nomination?

I decided to wait outside.

Dewey was waiting for me in his car. He put down the copy of *Dune* he had been reading. He'd been glued to it for days, was always glued to some book, none of which I ever had time to read. Nowadays I rarely read anything unless it might have a part in it for me. When I was a kid I read and read and read. And played *all* the parts.

"Hi, Beauty," Dewey said. "Congratulations on the nomination. It's fantastic."

"Thank you," I said.

"How does it feel?" he asked.

I had no reason to be anyone but myself with Dewey. "Dewey, I don't feel like talking. Could we just drive home quietly?"

"Okay, Princess. Anything the lady wants."

He turned on the radio and drove me home.

I opened the door to our house and, stepping inside, listened for the sound of the typewriter. No typing meant my mother had finished for the day or wasn't home. It was quiet in the house. As I walked toward the kitchen to get something to drink, I saw her in the living room. In our house the living room is the one place anyone rarely is. She must have actually been waiting for me to come home. I guess she'd heard.

"Hi," she said.

"Did you hear?" I asked.

"Ten people called me," she said.

"I hope it didn't ruin your afternoon's work."

"I could have unplugged the phone. I just kept count, that's all."

"Everyone's been nice about it," I said.

"They would be," she answered. That was another remark I knew would not be explained any further. I had grown adept, therefore, at ignoring such remarks.

"What's for dinner?" I asked.

"We're going to Phyllis's. Okay?"

"Great."

"How do you feel about the nomination, Kristin?"

"I want to win," I said.

"You might as well," she said, and went back to her room. There was another one-liner I didn't know exactly how to take.

"Change your clothes," she said from the doorway.

I went into my bedroom. There on the dresser, wrapped in gold paper, was a package that said "OPEN ME" on top of it. Inside was a beautiful cup in the shape of a unicorn, with a note inside in my mother's handwriting. It said, "Good luck." Sometimes I think she likes me.

[2] THE MYSTERY OF MY EXISTENCE

I will tell you what I know about it. The first time that this subject came up — as far as I can remember — I was about five years old and sitting on the stoop of our house in Brooklyn. A boy named Melvin, who was slightly older and bigger than I was, was sitting opposite me.

Quite suddenly he asked, "Where's your daddy?"

I didn't know. Nor could I remember having discussed it with my mother, but surely I must have asked her at some time, for I knew what to answer.

"He's dead," I said.

I went upstairs to my apartment. My mother, who in those days, before she wrote romances, brooded a lot, sat looking out the back window of her bedroom. The view was of the clothesline, but it truly was a comforting one. A bird might light on the line, and if two came on the line, it would grow taut, and when they flew off, the clothesline would wave. I guess I was a brooder, too, by blood, because I remember that over the years I, too, often sat and stared out that window.

I got a few peanut butter cookies out of the cookie jar and pulled a chair up next to my mother's.

"Want a cookie, Mommy?" I asked.

"Thank you, Kristin." She took one. "Did you put the lid back on the jar?"

"Yes," I said.

I sucked on my cookie and wondered how best to bring the subject up. Even at that age I was one for plunging in rather than beating around, so I said, "Where's my father?"

My mother never took her eyes off the clothesline, nor did I detect any change in the tone of her voice as she answered me: "You've asked me that before. He's dead."

"Do you know Melvin, from upstairs?" I asked. "He's five too."

"Don't think so," she said.

"He just asked me."

"What'd you say?"

"That my daddy was dead."

Now she looked at me. I knew by then, had been told repeatedly by relatives, that I had exactly her blue eyes, and I loved it when she really looked at me. Blues to blues.

"What did he say when you said that?"

"That his daddy was at work."

She laughed. "Really?"

"Yep,"I said.

"Well, it proves one thing," she said.

"What?"

"Some five-year-olds are a lot smarter than others."

And then she hugged me. Which she did not often do.

I do not know whether my mother knew then that I knew she was lying. I do know that I knew she was lying. How I knew I don't know.

After that, it seemed to me, the subject came up all the time, and, by the time I was in second grade, I simply needed more information.

"Mommy, what did my father die from?"

"Is somebody bothering you in school?"

"Everybody asks me sooner or later. Don't they ask you where your husband is?"

"No, they don't," she sighed.

"Well?"

"An automobile accident."

"Good," I said.

"Good? Kristin, what are you saying?"

"That's a good way for him to have died. It explains why it happened so young."

Blues to blues again.

"Yes, it does," she said.

"Someday will you tell me more about my father?"

"Yes, I will," she said.

"You promise?" I asked.

"Mothers don't need to make promises."

I never could figure out where she got her Rules and Standards for Motherhood from.

I really liked the automobile-accident story and I elaborated on it through the sixth grade. I kept to the basic premise, to which friends and teachers always responded with an appropriate sigh of sympathetic sadness.

I just changed details:

• A Porsche off a lonely cliff one night. An astronomer, he was headed toward his sky-high observatory.

• A Jaguar on the very day of a major auto race.

• A pickup truck which, as a stunt man in Hollywood, he was to get out of as it burned, but which accidentally crashed into a tree before it reached the place it was to burst into flames.

I stayed with the stunt man throughout the fifth and sixth grades. It had class. I added that my mother even had a movie of my father's pickup truck crashing. Anyone I told that one to always wanted to see the film.

"My mother says I'm not ready for it yet."

Sighs of sympathetic sadness.

The day I graduated from sixth grade I asked my mother again: "Are you ready to tell me more about my father?"

"It wouldn't be much of a graduation present," she answered.

"Yeah, it would," I stated firmly. "It would prepare me for junior high in California."

40

She was by now a successful writer. We were moving to California. Perhaps realizing that a new location would increase the number of people asking me questions, she decided to tell me more.

"We weren't married," she said.

I nodded and tried to issue a sigh of sympathetic sadness. I knew my mother much better by now than I had at five, and I could frequently get a glimpse of her real feelings.

"Before or after the crash?" I asked.

"Oh, Kristin," she said, laughing. "Neither." I could see she felt better. She knew me better now also, and I guess she knew I wouldn't push her on this subject anywhere she didn't want to go.

"Kristin, we would have married. In fact, he was killed the night he was coming to pick us up to take us to get married."

"Us?"

"You and me," she said.

"Of course," I said.

Now she turned dramatic on me, almost crying. "Had his car gotten a flat fifteen minutes later than it did, we would all have been killed together."

I wondered if I should offer her my stunt man story. She was an awful actress.

I got up and gave her a Kleenex. After she blew her nose, I said, "What luck."

"I suppose you could call it that," she said.

41

"What kind of work did he do?"

"He was a diamond merchant."

It was too much to let her get away with. After all, I was nearly twelve.

"A diamond merchant, Mother?" I knew there was irritation in my voice. "The main character in your third book was a diamond merchant."

"I didn't realize you'd read it," she said. "It was years ago."

Pause. I just waited.

"That character was modeled after your father."

She can't act, but she sure can think fast sometimes. I said I'd reread the book.

In junior high, teachers never asked and no children asked unless we were close friends. Half the people I knew in my junior high had no father at home and few of us wanted to talk about it.

So I let it wait. I now knew for a fact that I was illegitimate. About which nobody in my mother's family, including my mother, seemed to care. I still doubted the death of the diamond merchant, but it was not something I thought about a lot.

What I did think about quite often was what a real, live father might be like. It did seem an enviable situation, judging from those who had them.

In our apartment in Hollywood, where we lived while we looked for the house we now live in and while I began my acting career, I again approached my mother on the subject.

42

"What if I get interviewed?" I asked. "What should I say about my father?"

"What do you want to say?" she responded.

"That you're divorced and took back your maiden name."

"Okay," she said.

Now, you can imagine the freedom I felt. To invent my own father.

"I'm not sure at all about that look on your face, Kristin. Whatever you tell anyone, promise me you'll tell me."

Children do have to promise when asked.

"When are you going to tell me the truth?" I asked.

"I have. He's dead."

So I let it go. I thought occasionally about the deprived stunt man flying through the air, his last feeling regret that he would never see me. But I tried not to dwell on it. I had an accumulation of things not to dwell on and a special compartment in my head into which I put them. Sometimes I felt this patch of brain to be overcluttered and its contents clamoring to come out, but on the whole I found it best to leave it alone.

CLAPBOARD: ONCE UPON A GALAXY, SCENE 11

Most of that day my scenes were passive. My father had returned safely to us and we — my brother, sister and I — had greeted him. The children had gotten the presents that they had

43

asked for. In a corner of our rude shelter was the gold casket of jewels, opened, casting a glow that lit up the ruined insides of the old spaceship. I was going to get my rose. It was a big scene for me.

Father: Beauty? How beautiful this would look on you. *[Holds a shimmering necklace in front of her.]*

Beauty: *[Takes his hand and looks at him.]* Oh, Father. I am so glad you are back. *[Hesitates.]* Father, was it not summer where you were?

Father: *[Claps his hand to his tunic.]* I almost forgot. It's probably dead by now. *[Reaches inside his tunic and pulls out the rose, as perfect and fresh as when he left the Beast's garden. Hands it to Beauty.]*

Beauty: How lovely. How perfect. *[Throws her arms around her father.]* Oh, thank you. Thank you.

"Cut! Cut!"

I flinched. What was wrong now? I used to think I knew when I had done something well, but I no longer had the least idea.

Boone was coming toward me, shaking his head.

"Let's try this," he said finally. "Look at the rose for a long minute — maybe five seconds — then slowly lift your head and look at your father. Say 'Thank you' just once. VERY SOFTLY."

And of course it worked. A very real hush fell on the set and I could feel, back in the darkness,

44

people turning to watch us. It was more than the mechanical silence that the act of filming imposes on everyone present. It was a stillness and concentration of attention that is what an actor hopes to get. I loved the feeling. It washed over me. I glowed in it.

Boone could do that, at any rate. I guess it didn't matter that he wasn't too nice about it — or, rather, that he wasn't nice to me. We had the rest of the morning's shooting to do, and, still glowing, I decided that I could put up with Boone after all.

We continued with the scene.

Father: Don't thank me. I found not only riches but a beast.

Beauty: What do you mean by 'a beast,' Father?

Father: Well, a beast. Surely we've all known beasts. Ugly, horrible, frightening. Nothing like any one of us. And he wants you to go to him, Beauty. It is my punishment for stealing the rose.

Brother: *[Throwing his arms around Beauty.] No!* He can't have our Beauty.

Beauty: And if I don't go, Father?

Father: Then I must return to him forever.

Beauty: No! I will go.

Father: He is lonely. He wants only companionship.

Beauty: And you believed him?

Father: I believed him.

Beauty: *[Inhales deeply the fragrance of the rose and lifts her head.]* If you had not picked the

45

rose for me, it would not have happened. Of course I will go to the beast. And how terrible can it be, this place where roses grow?

"Cut! Print take four!" Boone hopped down and rushed toward us, beaming. "Beautiful. Perfect!" He turned to me and moved closer, and for a terrible second I thought he was going to hug me. I backed away involuntarily, hating myself the instant I did.

Boone stopped, rocked back on his stubby legs, looked up at me. He held out his hand and I handed him the rose. It was all I could think of to do. "Kristin," he said. I was transfixed by his beautiful blue eyes. "I actually believed you as a girl who would choose a place where roses grow." He turned and walked away, holding the rose.

I wandered back to my dressing room, thinking about Boone's last words. Why did it surprise him when I acted well? What did he expect?

We had finished a little earlier than expected. I changed my clothes, trading the artistically torn space costume for jeans and a shirt, and took off my make-up. I was supposed to take the bus home if I finished early, but I had decided that I would stay, at least for a while, to watch Keith's first big scene as the Beast. In that scene my father would pick the rose, the one he had already given me that morning. That kind of jumping back and forth in the story had confused me in my first movie, but I was used to it now.

Scenes are shot not as they appear in the final product, but as it is convenient to shoot them. It depends on the sets required, the schedules of the actors involved, the laws regulating work by minors, the availability of special equipment. In this case Keith was unavailable until the afternoon. In some ways *Galaxy* was more straightforward than my last movie, since there were so few sets and so few characters involved. In other ways it was worse, since so much of the really interesting part of the movie didn't actually "happen" at all, but was created somewhere else, by Boone's "magicians."

I found an inconspicuous spot at the back of the set to watch the next scene and I waited for the Beast — my leading man — to appear. It took so long for Keith to get into the Beast suit, and the suit was so hot and heavy and uncomfortable to wear, that there was a new urgency on the set. Boone, always meticulous, was even more determined to have everything just right.

The scene was outside the Beast's castle, which was on a planet just as bare and stricken as the one on which Beauty had been stranded. This worked out well, since both planets existed in the desert just outside Lancaster. But here there were just a gravel path and a backdrop.

Just then the big lights came on and I was plunged into deeper darkness. I hadn't heard Boone, but I saw him now, like a shadow himself, emerging from the dimness near me. I

47

shaded my eyes against the brightness of the lights. My father — Beauty's father, that is — was standing on the gravel path.

CLAPBOARD: ONCE UPON A GALAXY, SCENE 9

[Control Room: Watching Beauty's father, the Beast moves his hand over the controls. On the gravel path we see roses springing up. Close up, they burst into bud. A bud unfolds into a rose. Camera moves off. The bushes are covered with full red roses.]
"Action!"

My father lifted his head. The aroma of the roses reached him. He turned slowly and saw them. He went to them, bending his head to them. He was really very good. It was obvious that he was thinking of me, his beloved daughter. He glanced around, looked back at the roses, glanced around again and then, with a visible straightening of the shoulders, reached out and picked one of the roses.

And the Beast came out.

He came along the path, his great misshapen head swinging from side to side. I thought that the designers did a really good job with the Beast's head, giving it small, deep-set eyes, an elephantlike trunk, pointed ears and tortured lips. Everything was covered by wild tangles of fur!

Beast: *[Roaring.]* Is this the way you repay me? You steal a rose?

Father: *[Starting back in terror.]* It is just a rose.

Beast: I lodged you. Fed you. Gave you gifts of great splendor.

Father: *[Nodding. The rose has slipped from his fingers and lies on the gravel.]* You did, you did. I only wanted the rose for Beauty.

Beast: *[He has been slowly advancing on the frightened man, but stops at the word "Beauty" and tips his head.]* Yes, of course. Beauty. Your daughter.

"Cut! Cut!" Boone darted forward. The Beast's heavy head moved slowly to look at him.

"Walk toward me," Boone demanded. "You want to frighten me. Walk."

The Beast moved forward, his head bending gently as he moved, as if it were too heavy for his neck.

"Your head is *fantastic!*" Boone shouted. "Fantastic. But you walk like Kermit the Frog." The father actor giggled and I heard more laughter around me in the darkness. The Beast hung his head.

In the darkness even I wanted to laugh at the gesture. In that instant the Beast became Keith in a beast suit, acting chagrined. I was pretty sure that he wasn't. I chagrined a lot more easily than Keith.

"You are not a frog," Boone continued more softly. "You are a *beast*. Watch me."

He stepped back between the roses and was instantly out of sight. Then he came out, hanging his head in shy imitation of Keith's chagrin. The Beast laughed.

Boone stood very still for a moment until everyone was watching him. I strained my eyes to see past the jungle of cables and cameras and booms and light standards.

"Walk like me," he said and started to walk. It was just his ordinary walk, but slower, and it was the right way for the Beast to walk. The Beast came to stand beside him, and they walked together across the stage, back and forth, the Beast's walk becoming more and more labored, until at last Boone said, "That's it. That's it."

I was glad that I was back in the darkness, that no one knew I was watching. Because the simplest, most elementary thing had just occurred to me, something that everyone else there had surely known from the first day. Boone *knew* how he looked when he walked. He *knew* it was the walk of a beast. I felt small and awful. Keith could stand up straight when the scene was over and stride away on his strong legs. Boone had to walk like that. Always. Forever. And the way he walked had bothered me. I went out, away from the shadows, away from the set, away from Boone, trying not to think of the way I walked, of my legs moving easily beneath me, carrying me away from something I did not want to face.

Outside in the sunlight — it was very early

afternoon — my face burned. I hoped that no one had seen my sly little imitations of Boone-walking, the ones I had been so proud of. If no one had seen them, then no one would know what an ignorant person I was. Making fun of something I knew nothing about. I decided to do something about my ignorance.

I caught the 37 bus. As I got on I found myself turning to the people sitting on the brown vinyl seats and smiling at them.

Nobody smiled back.

Nobody recognized me.

I was used to that, although I hoped it was going to change any day now. When I won the Emmy. Winning the Emmy would say that I am a good actress, which is important to me — I am pretty sure I *am* a very good actress — but more, it would tell everybody, This is Kristin Kelley. She is important.

Everywhere I went, people would know me. My mother is famous; millions of people know her name. Right now somewhere in the world someone is saying, "Here's the new Amanda Crayne book." But my mother can take the bus or go to the market and no one knows who she is. Writers can do that, and so can painters — be the best at what they do, be famous and anonymous at the same time.

I wouldn't want that. Maybe that's why I want to be an actress. Not that I don't love acting. I love the special feeling of creating a person who isn't me but who is real and believable to an audience. I love being swept away by someone else's emotions and life, of being moved out of myself for the time I am acting. But in acting, your fame *is* your face and body and voice. And when you're good and you're successful, everybody knows you. And that's what I want: to be famous, to be recognized.

Did Boone ever think of that? After all, people were going to look at him no matter what. Did he decide that if he was going to be stared at anyway, he might as well be stared at and recognized?

What, I wondered, would it be like to look like Boone and not to hide? What was it like to be a dwarf? Why was he a dwarf? Had he always been that way? I tried to imagine a dwarf baby, but it was too much for me to picture.

The bus swung down Wilshire, past the tall apartment buildings, the condominiums. I wasn't going home to Santa Monica right away. I was going to UCLA, to the library, to find out about dwarfs. Or dwarves. I didn't even know the proper plural.

I got off and started the long trek to the library. I had come here often with my mother. There are times she barely knows I live in the same house, and then there come times when she wants me with her everywhere she goes. And frequently she's researching something and I get to browse in the library or hang out in the quad at UCLA and look at the people.

Nothing gives my mother the pleasure that her research does, and nothing gives me the pleasure that looking at people does. Her specialty is historical romance, and I have seen her research eighteenth-century England, second-century Greece, fourteenth-century Russia. I expect her to do seventeenth-century Alaska next. In all centuries love makes the world go around.

She is methodical about her research. She takes the books to a faraway carrel, sets them up in Library of Congress order, puts her paperweight (she always has a paperweight in her purse) against the books as a book end. She then takes out her red Pilot pen, her blue Pilot pen, her three sharpened pencils, her note pad and miscellaneous scraps of paper to be used as bookmarks.

Then she turns to me, as though I were part of the entire process and simply the last thing to be taken care of. "I'll be three hours, Kristin. Here is ten dollars. Eat something, look at your watch, find something to read, do not converse with professors wandering the grounds. Real professors do not wander the grounds or want to talk to small children. Come back in three hours."

I enjoy the ritual and know that for three hours she will work among ancient records until she knows where her setting is, who her characters are (or will be) or how they met — details that set her rummaging and rummaging deeper and deeper into her books.

I really think she's happiest in her three-hour research stints. There are no people she cannot control, no decision that doesn't swing her way, no life-threatening situations that cannot be relieved.

I think writers have an easy life. Nothing even to memorize; you just make it up yourself. She says actors and actresses couldn't possibly create a character without the writer's skill. She doesn't really believe the characters need the actors even. Says it just worked out that way. Can't put all those people together in the theater and just have them read. But otherwise, actors and actresses are unnecessary beings.

Tact is not my mother's strongest point.

Nor is it mine.

The UCLA hours are some of my favorite times with Mother. I use the ten dollars and three hours in so many ways. There's bowling, wandering the arcade, buying shirts, looking for disreputable professors (if they follow me, I run away. None of them can run), eating at the cafeteria, looking through the bookstore, walking around, sneaking into lecture halls. College lecturers are really much more interesting than set or high school teachers.

But today, alone on my own mission, I felt

almost as if I were my mother. *I* was doing the research. On Adam Michael Boone.

I first climbed the steps to the university library. So many handsome boys and slim, beautiful girls, some going up the steps with books under their arms, some coming down the steps with books in their arms.

And all the faces different. How can there be so many different faces? When I hear numbers concerning stars and galaxies, I become conscious in a different way, aware of something so far too big to be understood that it is more like a place one enters than a thought in your head. Well, faces do that to me too. Not always, but often. Here I was, me with my face, going up the stairs and they, strangers with their faces, coming down toward me.

When this hits me, as it did this day, I always investigate my thinking as far as I can, and right now my feeling was that I wanted to *be* all those faces.

Of course I couldn't be. But perhaps I could act them all, one way or the other, someday.

Just as I reached the door to the library, I saw this boy whose nose I'd like to be. That thought jolted me back to whatever this place called reality is. It almost made me laugh at myself, since one of my greatest faults is that I take myself so seriously.

Once inside, ready to work, I transformed

myself into a twenty-one-year-old coed with a heavy paper due. I don't know if anyone else saw me that way, but it was who I was then on the library set.

I approached the reference desk. "Where can I find a book on medical terms?"

"In particular, for instance, what do you want to know?"

He was about twenty-two, a graduate student, well cast, handsome and clean-cut, but would not take the viewer's mind off the action.

"In particular, for instance, just a book on medical terminology."

"Perhaps, little girl" (— wrong, I was wrong. God, was he miscast —), "if you tell me what you want to look up, I can help you."

"All right," I said. "Measles."

"Measles?"

"Yes," I said, nodding solemnly.

"What do you want to know about measles?" he asked.

"Their ionic composition," I said still more solemnly, confidingly even.

He seemed struck. He had at last realized that this conversation was getting out of his depth.

"Here, let me get you a book that will help."

"That'd be sweet of you," I said.

He walked away efficiently and rapidly and returned as quickly. "Just gone a flash," he said.

"So true," I said.

"May I see your library card?" he asked.

56

I hated this part. I produced my mother's ID.

"Oh, wow. Is Amanda Crayne your mother? I read all her books."

"Yes," I said. "She is."

"They're such great background for some of my own work."

"Good," I said.

He hesitated. "They always let you use the books?"

"Oh, sure," I said (humbly sweet smile here). "Everybody knows my mom around here."

"Well, here you are."

He handed me *Taber's Cyclopedic Medical Dictionary.*

I went over to a seat near the far windows, as far from other people as possible. I wanted a little privacy. I looked up "dwarf." I found:

> **dwarf** [AS. *dweorg,* dwarf]. An abnormally short or undersized person; a pygmy.
>
> *d., achondroplastic.* One with normal trunk but possessing shortened extremities with a large head, and protruding buttocks.
>
> *d., asexual.* One with deficient sexual development.
>
> *d., hypophyseal.* One due to hypofunction of anterior lobe of the hypophysis.
>
> *d., infantile.* One showing marked physical, mental and sexual underdevelopment.
>
> *d., Levi-Lorain.* An hypophyseal or pituitary d.
>
> *d., micromelic.* One with very small limbs.
>
> *d., ovarian.* An undersized female due to absence or underdevelopment of the ovaries.

d., phocomelic. One with abnormally short diaphyses of either pair of extremities or of all four.

d., physiologic. A person normally developed except for stature.

d., pituitary. An hypophyseal one.

d., primordial. One in whom there is a selective deficiency of growth hormone but with otherwise normal endocrine function.

d., rachitic. One due to rickets.

d., renal. One due to renal osteodystrophy.

d., thanatophoric. SEE: *thanatophoric dwarfism.*

I read them all, although before I was through I was fairly certain my director was an achondroplastic dwarf. "Physiologic dwarf," I guessed, was a midget.

I read a little more:

Dwarfism. Condition of being abnormally small. May be hereditary, or a result of endocrine dysfunction, deficiency diseases, renal insufficiency, diseases of the skeleton or other causes.

But then there was no more information in that book. I gave the book back to the historically romantic grad student and followed him to the section he'd taken it from. I went through all the titles but found nothing.

I went to the medical library. Here I decided not to ask any questions — I didn't believe I looked like a medical student — and tried to find my way among the catalogues.

I found my information in J.A. Balen's *Dispro-portionate Short Stature:*

> *Prognosis:* Achondroplastic dwarfs are usually hearty individuals in whom a normal life span can be expected. They are also unusually strong for their size and quite agile, and they tend to lead a physically active life. However, in 40% of adults (usually males) the prognosis is compromised by the cauda equina syndrome resulting from spinal stenosis.

Whatever "cauda equina syndrome resulting from spinal stenosis" was, I hoped it wasn't catching. I was getting nervous about finding out exactly what the book meant. Nervous for Boone. And very uncomfortable about the whole thing.

Next book: Alfred Vogl, *The Fate of the Achondroplastic Dwarf: Neurologic Complications of Achondroplasia.*

In this book there was a picture of a statue of a dwarf who lived around 2700 BC. They even knew his name: Chnoumhotep. He'd been an officer under the pharaohs. The picture of the statue only looked a little like Boone, for Boone's head was slightly larger and his body slightly thinner. But the proportions were the same.

As I read, I felt physically uncomfortable, and I began to wish I didn't have access to the accumulated literature of the UCLA libraries. Or even a library card.

We can be sure that he was an achondroplastic dwarf. We must assume that he had outstanding abilities but we do not know how long he lived and from what illness he died. From the appearance of the statuette, it seems that he was in the prime of his life when he was called to join his ancestors and there is a good chance that he may have fallen victim to the fate that threatens all achondroplastic dwarfs from the day of their birth, and that he, too, may have become paralyzed from his waist down.

I read only a little more:

. . . certain skeletal changes inherent in the achondroplastic dwarf predispose the affected individuals to progressively crippling and even life threatening lesions of the spinal cord, from paraparesis to quadriplegia . . .

That was enough. As I was reading I had begun to see Adam Michael Boone more clearly. He'd been born that way. When did his mother notice? I wondered. Could you tell instantly when the doctor held the baby aloft to cut the umbilical cord? Or later? I closed the book. I'd certainly found a lot more than I'd been looking for. Damn.

What had I been looking for?

I kept asking myself that as I put the books away, got myself together and left the building.

It was getting late, and I walked up to the place in front of Murphy Hall where my mother often took me to see the sunset. Usually I don't care about sunsets. Beautiful, true, but not like stars, uncountable, or faces, unpredictable. But today I wanted to see the sunset. And it did its number for me, going from oranges through reds and then into deep black, and I was still standing there, a little cold now with the sun gone down.

What had I come looking for?

Knowledge is power. That's why I'd come. Just in case I might find some special information to use in working with Adam Michael Boone, whom I found so incredibly preposterous to work for. Impossible even to talk to.

Well, I certainly had my information. "The prognosis is compromised by the cauda equina syndrome resulting from spinal stenosis," or in words I could grasp, "the fate that threatens all achondroplastic dwarfs from the day of their birth . . . that he, too, may have become paralyzed from his waist down."

It echoed and just kept echoing.

Not altogether pleased with my research, I started walking toward the bus stop. It was dark now and all the faces looked the same.

FLASHBACK: MORE ON THE MYSTERY OF MY EXISTENCE

My mother said that it looked like we had it made financially. Her earnings could buy us a new house and keep us in reasonable style, and my earnings would take care of college if I wanted to go and any dental work I might ever need. She deeply appreciated, she told me once, that I had not needed orthodontic work before her fifth book was published.

And so we found this marvelous house in Santa Monica, where we still live today. It was on moving day that I began to come closer to discovering who my father was. It was through both carelessness and trust on my mother's part that I got my next information. And more even than that.

"There are ten filing cabinets, Kristin. They will be moved by the movers, but we need to empty the drawers into these boxes. You get to do that."

"Mother, when Julie moved they just took the whole filing cabinet, drawers, files and all."

"Kristin, Julie had Bekins. In the interest of the house payment, I have hired three boys from Santa Monica Community College. They have a truck. They said to empty the cabinets. It's not that big a job. Okay?"

"Okay," I said.

I had never gone through my mother's files. Perhaps had there been just one filing cabinet I would have been curious, but with ten filing cabinets I guess I thought they all held rough drafts of her books or future notes or whatever. She had told me once that a writer should never throw anything away. Everything may turn up in a book.

She had also told me never to read anybody else's mail or papers lying around on their desks, but I had always known that I would do that if ever the opportunity presented itself, although there'd never been anybody else's mail I'd wanted to go to all the trouble of steaming open.

She'd also taught me not to open people's chest drawers, look in their medicine cabinets or ask questions about their religion. None of that came up often in my life.

So, therefore, up to this very afternoon of opening the first of the ten cabinets — that's forty drawers of folders that writers should never throw away — I had a clean record.

For a while it looked as if it would stay that way. The first thirty-six boxes got filled with stuff from the books she had written or was planning to write. The last cabinet was another story. The file folders were all pink and the very first was marked "PERSONAL." I wondered how much time I had before Santa Monica Community College sent its three strongest men to move our house.

My mother looked in. "How are you doing?"

"Mother, wouldn't you consider throwing some of this stuff away?"

"My dear Kristin, I'm only thirty-three years old. I wouldn't consider throwing anything away. When I'm eighty I'm going to reread it all."

"Mother, I dropped a folder and when I picked it up I saw that it said 'CARS.' And as I put the stuff back in, I saw that it had a bill in it for fixing your 1972 Pontiac, which you no longer have. At eighty, surely that will have lost some interest."

She looked me steadily in the eye. "Kristin, you do not have the writer's mind. Who is to know what I will make out of that bill for the Pontiac? Have faith, please, baby. Don't throw anything away, don't read anything and be glad you're an actress, for, as I say, you don't have the writer's mind."

I sort of felt sorry for her, because it was obvious to me that I had the criminal's mind. She left the room and I continued reading the headings on the personal files. They were "CARS," "BILLS," "DOCTORS," "HAIR," "MOVIE REVIEWS," "PROTEST LETTERS," "CHARITIES," "CONFERENCES," "SPEECHES I'LL MAKE SOMEDAY," "TO FORGET" and on and on. I had a few thoughts of my own on things to look for if she truly kept everything, so I tried to find "FATHER," "LOVE LETTERS," "HATE LETTERS" (there was a "FAN LETTERS"), "MEN I HAVE KNOWN," "THE PAST" and a few others. Everything looked fascinating, but the movers would be in soon. I reminded myself that now that I had a place and reason to be dishonest, I could continue my search after our move, but one never knows when decency will strike one, so I just pressed on. There was no file marked "KRISTIN" and that in itself was a disappointment.

The strangest one I found before I hit pay dirt was called "ANTIDOTE TO DISMAY AT THE NATURE OF THE UNIVERSE." I wouldn't have missed it. It was the kind of heading I liked to give things. Not often, but every once in a while, I thought I could prove in a court of law that we were related, that she truly was my mother. This kind of thing counted heavily as proof. In the folder were clippings and cartoons and typed-up quotations.

I would go back to that file sometime. I just knew it. But I guessed that except for this find I might as well have been honest. I kneeled and started to put the personals into the boxes waiting for them.

Pay dirt: Folder marked "PHYLLIS."

I opened it and my heart started beating strangely. Oh, my wonderful mother. Not just letters from Phyllis, but carbons of your letters to her. Vanity or forgetfulness? She had always said she had a bad memory, but with hundreds of characters that she remembered every detail about, I found that hard to believe. Vanity.

The first one was dated November 10, 1967.

Dear Phyllis,

Thank God I have you to write to. The worst is over now. There were only a few bad moments really I think. My mother had pointed out — you remember her flair for realism — that if I had come home to have a baby I'd have to expect the neighbors would notice. And certainly my relatives. I had to admit that was likely. The neighbors she didn't think we needed to tell — they could just play among themselves and see who figured it out first.

The family, my parents insisted, should be told. Immediately. Especially since we might need to borrow money from Uncle Stephen. So he shouldn't be the last to know.

She called everybody up. Come over for dinner Saturday. Amanda's home. We have something to tell you. So they came. All agreed I looked wonderful and, if I was going to live in New York, that was wonderful, and who needed Hollywood anyway and if anyone didn't realize what a talent I had, they should be beaten, but WHY HAD I COME HOME?

"That's an interesting question," I said.

"You don't have to answer if you don't want to," my suddenly cowardly father said.

"Listen, I came 3000 miles for this question," I said.

Phyllis, you remember Uncle Harry. He's the one who works in the mental institution. Remember? He wanted to take me there for a tour on my ninth birthday, but I said I wouldn't go unless you came and my father said we'd both prefer the zoo. Remember? High-pitched voice, skinny, moustache. The one who's not Uncle Stephen, who took us both to the circus. Okay?

Uncle Harry said, "You got the question. What's the answer?"

"I'm pregnant."

"But you're only nineteen," my Aunt Edna said.

"It can work out that way," my mother said.

Silence. Then the real bad few minutes. As if I hadn't thought it all through for myself.

Uncle Harry: "How many months pregnant are you, Amanda?"

"About three," I said.

He thought for a moment. Nobody in the room breathed, I swear.

"That's not too old . . . I mean, too late," he said, and there was this continued silence. Not a word from anyone.

"No, Uncle Harry. I don't think that's too old (and I emphasized the TOO), or too late. I still think there's a good chance we can get him or her into a good college. So he can make something of himself or herself."

Uncle Stephen, God bless him, roared with laughter. Then my folks laughed. And Uncle Stephen said, "I'm not promising to put anyone through college before I know if he or she can play football, but I'd love to handle the delivery costs."

Then I started to cry.

"Please, not one of those pregnancies," my father said.

Finally, they all went home.

We all three (four?) cleaned up together. I had by this time stopped crying.

When I was in bed later, my mother said,

67

actually tucking me into bed (which I think she should stop doing soon), "I'm glad that's over and done with."

"It was always your choice, you know that," my father said, standing at my bedside. "We would have gone either way."

"Yes," I said, settling back into the pillows. "I know."

So, Phyl, everybody's about to be an illegitimate grandparent, or granduncle, or grandaunt. This baby had better take after my family.

I'm counting on papa's genes being weaker than mine. He throws them around so.

Write to me about Hollywood.

Love, your friend,
Amanda

Dear Amanda,

I love your Uncle Stephen. Your Uncle Harry is a creep. Always was. I knew they'd all want the baby. Your mother always wanted more babies, and my mother always promised her she'd have grandchildren. See? I told my mom you're pregnant and she said, "Wonderful! Don't you do it."

Fat chance of me doing it. I'm working forty hours a day to build up my agency. I have to walk all over the studios visiting casting directors. You have to know everybody in the business in order to know the right person at the right time.

I have six clients now — and got jobs for three of them. Commercials. But we're all start-

*ing someplace. Have your baby and come back
and be my client.*

Love,
Phyllis

Dear Phyllis,

*Sorry I haven't written lately. I'm so busy
reading books about babies. They do all the
things we do, only smaller, and I am trying to be
ready to handle everything before May 31, the
target date.*

*I don't want to come back to be an actress.
Look at the kind of people you meet being an
actress. I'm going to be a writer and live in New
York and work out of the baby's nursery —
that's six feet at the end of my bedroom.*

*You should be dating, not walking around in
the hot California sun.*

Love,
Amanda

Dear Amanda,

*I'm getting married. He's thirty-three, hand-
some and a casting director. His name is Martin
Eglin. He's wonderful.*

*We'll get married in May! Guess where.
Right. He went to Erasmus too. So we'll see you
soon.*

*By the way, Prince Charming was one of my
six clients. Every time I saw him he'd ask about
you and I'd pitch him some lie or other. Finally I
decided to ditch him. I'm not his agent anymore.
He's #1 in my dead file.*

Will you never tell him?
Will he never know?

> Love,
> Phyllis

Dear Phyllis,
HURRAH! CONGRATULATIONS.
Do it in early May. At the rate I'm growing I wouldn't be able to fit into a chair at the reception. And I sure want to be there.
In answer to your questions about deadbeat: He will never know if he has to learn it from me. As far as I know that just leaves you to keep a secret.
His existence stirs not a pang of interest in me. I think about his chromosomes a lot, though. See you soon.

> Love,
> Amanda

Then I found telegrams and their carbons. Wow!

BABY, KRISTIN KELLEY, BORN MAY 15. 6 LBS, 3 OZ. STUNNINGLY BEAUTIFUL. LOOKS LIKE ALL MY GENES. WE'LL BOTH BE AT THE WEDDING. AMANDA

IF SHE'S THAT BEAUTIFUL, I'LL SIGN HER WHEN WE GET TO NEW YORK AND I'LL MAKE HER A STAR. LOVE. SEE YOU ON THE 25TH. PHYLLIS AND MARTIN

End of letters in that file.

I couldn't wait to find the next ones.

My mother appeared in the doorway. "Kristin, are you reading material in the folders?"

"Certainly not," I said.

"Then what is taking you so long?"

"Resting from bending over so much," I answered. "I'll hurry."

"Well, do," she said, and walked back out.

I hurried and I kept thinking, Who was Prince Charming? Besides this, though, I had an unusual feeling of what I can only describe as joy. My mother had certainly done quite a few things, hard things, just right — and just for me.

CLAPBOARD: ONCE UPON A GALAXY, SCENE 14

[Beast, Beauty's father and Beauty stand in the big hall of the Beast's castle. Father shimmers, fades and is gone. Beauty turns to the Beast and begins to cry.]

Beast: Do not cry. While he disappears here, he appears elsewhere. He will be on Earth again, safe with your brother and sister.

"Cut! Keith, that was very nice, but isn't it a strange line to deliver to a young lady who is not crying?"

Keith shrugged and I spoke: "I was hoping you hadn't noticed."

"Very funny, Kristin." Boone came to the center of the set. "But not funny enough to bring

71

any of us to tears, so the humor, as well as our time, is wasted."

I said nothing.

"Well? Can you cry?"

Why on earth couldn't I cry? I always could before.

"I don't seem to be able to right now."

Nobody was talking. Everybody was listening to Boone make a fool out of me.

"All actresses can cry," Boone said.

I didn't answer him. I actually was on the verge of tears from the embarrassment he was causing me, but he couldn't be expected to see that.

He came closer. It shocked me each time we stood this close that I was actually the taller of us. His head back, his blue eyes sought my clear, untear-stained ones. He looked deeply at me, icily, I swear it.

"Actresses, Miss Kelley, can cry when it is necessary. If you cannot cry when all around you are waiting for you to cry, then you are a failure. Do you think it possible that you could get up there now and think of some manner in which to make yourself cry? I leave it to you."

He turned and walked back to the chair he sat in. Everything waited on me.

I turned to Keith, whose head must have been roasting by now under all that heavy gear. "I'm ready."

And this time when the Beast made my father disappear, I looked over at Boone, who had sat in his chair and was now leaning forward, his chin resting on his hands, and my tears started to flow. "Sleep," the Beast said, "and your tears will cease to flow." I lay down and reminded myself that all actresses can also stop crying.

Boone looked pleased. I knew that he thought he had made me cry by embarrassing me. But ultimately I had had to do the trick myself and I did it by asking myself how I would feel if I woke up one morning and looked like Boone. I thought that I ought to tell him that one for his repertory of methods on how to work with child actresses, but I was afraid to.

Later, when we had finished and I had changed my clothes and was leaving, Boone stopped me. "There was a phone call for you. Dewey can't meet you."

"Guess it's the bus then," I said.

"No," Boone said. "It's me."

"You?"

"Yes. Dewey called your mother. She called me because she couldn't make it either."

"I'm sorry," I said. He deserved at least that. Only my mother thought of directors as pinch-hitting chauffeurs.

"It's okay," he said, and he laughed.

In the car I sat on the plush front seat and relaxed back.

"Put your seat belt on," he said.

"Right," I said.

His setup was really interesting, but I did not want to stare.

"You can stare," he said. "I am lucky enough to have a brother who's an engineer, and when Chrysler said they couldn't build me a car for a price I could pay, my brother showed them how to do it."

What his brother had created was a second layer of car, which appeared after the midsection, so that where I sat everything was in regular proportions. Where Boone sat, he was level with me, but from there down the car resembled a child's toy, except that every detail — brakes, gears, everything he had to touch to run the car — was professionally tooled. So that rather than a child's toy, the car brought to mind special equipment and almost a sense of envy that all the devices this car had, your own would never have.

Boone laughed again. "That's the longest anyone ever stared," he said. "Good for you."

If I have not mentioned Boone's laugh before, it is because I had never admitted before to myself how much I liked it. He really laughed with such happiness in his voice that you thought the sound ought to be the pattern for everyone's laughter. And why he laughed so much was way beyond me.

"I like cars," I said.

"Too bad you're not older. I'd let you take a crack at driving this."

"A 'crackup' would be better wording, don't you think?"

"I do. Yes."

I guessed then that Boone had a great need to get his handicap out in the open, to show people that it ought not to be a serious enough issue to block communication between them. This didn't work with me. I did not feel one bit more at ease with his poor warped body than I had before I got into his perfectly constructed motor world. I knew I needed to pretend to be at ease, that he needed that, but I didn't know how. Maybe someday he'd teach me how to act that scene. For now, I was just glad we were getting close to my house. I wanted to get out and run on my perfect legs until I was out of breath.

"This is it," Boone said, pulling up in front of my house. "Yes," I said, and we said our good nights and I ran into the house and yelled to my mother that I'd be right back and I went out again to do my running.

When I returned I saw that Phyllis and my mother were on the couch in the living room, chatting. Phyllis, as far as I know, is the only one my mother ever "chats" with and the only one she ever sits in the living room with. Even before I'd read the letters, I'd known that theirs was a special kind of friendship. I always had the feeling they were two girls getting together after school instead of two mothers. I have always tried to overhear their conversations whenever I could.

Seeing them together, I went upstairs, washed and changed as quickly as I could and returned to the top stair, where I could listen without being observed. I had no friend I talked to the way they talked. I think I listened just so I'd know how to play such a scene if it ever came up on a job.

Tonight they were talking about Chinese food. They would just mention a restaurant name and, for no reason apparent to me, suddenly go off into gales of laughter. The funniest Chinese restaurants, I concluded, were those eaten in during their twelfth grade in high school. I was making a mental note of that when the doorbell rang.

I could just see the doorway from my post without being seen. Looking through the peephole, my mother yelled through the door, "Larry who? TV what?" Then, "Do come in."

She opened the door. I immediately recognized the tone. It was the same one she'd used when being interviewed after winning her Romance Writers of America award.

Boy, was it something to get nominated for an Emmy. They even came after me at home. But this was not the case. Larry Winter wanted to interview my mother. About me. Poor man, I thought, he's about to be thrown out. But I was wrong again. I can never predict my mother's behavior. That had its disadvantages, but on the other hand, she is never dull to be with or to watch in action.

"Do come in," she said again. The gracious Writer at Home. I watched them walk into the living room, Larry taking out a notebook.

"Phyllis, I want you to meet Larry Winter. He's from *TV World* and is here to interview me about Kristin."

Phyllis rose from the couch, as though on cue. "I really must be going then and leave the two of you to talk."

"Sit down, Phyllis," my mother commanded, and I knew Phyllis would sit right down. "I wouldn't dream of having you go. You know the theater world so much better than I." Then she introduced Phyllis to Larry Winter as "my dearest friend, Phyllis Star, of whom of course you've heard."

"Of course," Larry said. "The agent. I'm happy to meet you. I do believe you sent Kristin on that first milk commercial when she wasn't interested in acting at all."

I winced. But good friend Phyllis. She could have been on the stage. She said, "Oh, did Kristin tell you that story?"

"Yes," he said. "She was quite enthusiastic about you."

"I'm so glad," Phyllis said. "Well, you two just talk away."

77

"Why don't we get started, then?" my mother said.

"Right," Larry said.

My mother and Phyllis sat back. I leaned forward.

"Mrs. Kelley, I believe you are also an artist. A writer."

"Oh, I am, Larry. You don't mind if I call you Larry, do you?"

"No, no. Please do."

"Let's not waste time on my work. Let's just talk about Kristin. She's the most important star in the family just now."

"Yes, well, I was hoping to get some background. I've talked to her about her career and her feelings about the Emmy. She explained that she never had been interested in acting before that day in your office, Phyllis, but I was wondering if you, Mrs. Kelley, as her mother, had noticed her talent before then."

"Oh, yes, certainly I had," my mother said. "She has always been gifted at everything she has chosen to do. I doubt if she remembers it, but when I first began writing she used to dress up as a princess or a housemaid or whomever I was writing about and act out the parts."

"How young was she then?"

"Not quite five. Kristin's always been incredibly precocious."

"You were home with her, then, when she was a child?"

78

"Well, certainly," my mother said. "I believe a mother should be in the home. Don't you?"

"Well," Larry said. He paused. "Some mothers, of course, have to work outside their homes. When were you divorced, Mrs. Kelley? I mean, at what age did Kristin no longer have two parents in the home?"

I leaned so far forward that I nearly fell.

"Well, she never had two parents in the home. Her father always went to work."

"I see. What did Mr. Kelley do?" he asked.

She sighed, threw up her hands in a gesture of, of-course-Larry-would-understand-why-they-were-no-longer-married. "He was totally dull, I'm afraid. He sold insurance, all sorts — life, auto, home, theft, fire. He tried to keep it interesting, but insurance has just never thrilled me. He was very successful and, I assure you, a good father, but, well, I just couldn't stand hearing about premiums every night at dinner. And I didn't think that sort of thing was good for Kristin. All that talk of tragedy, you know."

Larry nodded. "How old was Kristin when you ended your marriage?"

"Five," my mother said. "One night when I was tucking her in, she said to me, 'Tell me that story Daddy tells about the man whose house burned down and he would have lost everything except that the good fairy had given him an insurance policy with my daddy's company.' I filed the next day."

Larry nodded, transfixed. "Whatever made you marry him?" he asked, swept away by the story. "I mean, not that it's any of my business."

"I was a foolish young thing," my mother said. Boone should have heard that delivery.

It stopped Larry from that line of questioning. "I see."

"And, of course, Kristin was meant to be. I do believe in those things, don't you?"

"Oh, yes," Larry said.

"Do you have any other questions about Kristin?" my mother asked.

"Do you want her to keep up a career in acting? Do you feel it's a secure career for her? Do you have any other ambitions for her?"

"I think Kristin is destined to be one of America's greatest actresses," my mother said. I hoped they didn't hear my sharp intake of breath. "Otherwise, I would hope that she would be a librarian. I think that's a solid occupation. But as it is, I think fame has marked her for its own."

He's about to realize she's putting him on, I thought. Surely. But Larry *TV World* was still writing everything down. He looked up now and smiled. "Well, I think I've got enough now to round out my story. It will probably be a feature — if she wins the Emmy, of course."

I realized then that the interviews had only been conducted in case I won.

80

"Of course," my mother said.

Larry stood. "Oh," he said as he neared the door, "I might want to contact Kristin's father if I do a longer piece sometime. Where is he now?"

"Dead," my mother said. "A skiing accident."

"Oh, I'm sorry."

"Don't be. He was insured," she said.

Larry smiled and left more rapidly than he had entered.

And then, through the laughter that instantly suffused them both the second Larry was out the door, came the answer to the interview question that hadn't been asked.

Phyllis gave it.

"Oh, my God, Amanda, Howard selling life insurance," she said. "Oh, my God."

My mother, laughing as hard as I've ever heard her, told Phyllis, "We shouldn't laugh. What if he sees it in print? I may have gone too far."

"He's at the Ahmanson, you know."

My mother gasped through her laughter: "You're kidding. Doing what?"

"Peregrine in *Volpone*."

"Again!"

"Yes," Phyllis said, laughing. "Again."

"Well," my mother sighed, "I may indeed have gone too far."

Just far enough, Mother. Just far enough. Howard Peregrine, here I come.

CLAPBOARD: ONCE UPON A GALAXY, SCENE 25

On the set the next day, having discovered the accessibility of my father, I was unexpectedly clumsy. I did not want my emotions to affect me this way. I did not believe an actor should let anything affect his or her performance. But when I moved during make-up and caused the make-up artist to drop her eye shadow, I knew that I'd have to be extra careful in front of the camera.

[An alcove in the castle: A table is set for two, silver and crystal gleam in the candlelight. Beauty and the Beast face each other across the table.]

Beast: I particularly like violin music, Beauty. Do you?

[Violin music fills the air.]

Beauty: *[Lifts her head at the sound of the music.]* How lovely!

Beast: *[Lifting a bottle in his hands.]* More champagne, Beauty?

Beauty: *[Raises her glass to be filled.]* Please.

I raised the glass to my lips, or at least halfway to my lips. It slipped from my fingers and hit the tabletop, shattering into a mass of bubbles and broken glass.

"Cut! Cut! CUT!"

People appeared. They had the difficult task of taking everything off the table because neither Keith nor I dared step from the table until the broken glass was cleared away. A hair dryer was turned on my wet dress.

"Kristin," Boone asked, "would you like a stunt woman for this scene?"

Everybody laughed. I made a face at Boone, grateful for his humor. "I think I can handle it."

Beast: More champagne, Beauty?

Beauty: Please.

Beast: Would you like to walk with me in the garden?

Beauty: *[Rises from her chair.]* I'd like that.

[Beast rises and goes to her side and together they leave the alcove.]

I heard the laughter before I heard Boone shouting *"Cut!"* and I looked back. The Beast was bent over, his shoulder almost to the level of my waist. I turned and a muffled cry of pain came from the Beast. From Keith. Somehow — I have no idea how — one of Beauty's flashing rings had gotten itself wound in part of the Beast's tangled, flowing hair. As soon as I realized what had happened, I raised my hand so that Keith could stand up straight. Someone came and disengaged the ring from the Beast.

Boone was still sitting with his chin on his hands. He got off the chair and came toward us slowly, shaking his head from side to side. "You're a hard woman to woo, Kristin."

I actually hung my head.

"You come here and sit down, and I'll do your part." He raised his hand warningly and,

83

laughing, said, "If you think you can get safely from there to here." Boone stopped me as I passed, took the offending ring from my finger and slipped it on his hand. "Now *I* am Beauty," he said.

I went to Boone's chair and sat down. I noticed that people were drifting over to watch, people who did not normally watch the shooting.

Beast: More champagne, Beauty?

Beauty: Of course, Beastie, love. *(Before the Beast could move, Boone-Beauty reached over the table and picked up the bottle. He lifted it to his lips and drank.)*

I heard the whirr of machinery and realized that the cameras were running.

Beast: Would you like to walk with me in the garden, Beauty?

Beauty: *[Springing to his feet and bouncing.]* I thought you'd *never* ask! *(The Beast rose and as he emerged from behind the table, Boone-Beauty launched himself from the ground, flying straight upward. The Beast caught him in both arms. Boone-Beauty rested his head against the Beast suit.)*

Beauty: *[Continues.]* You walk. I'll ride.

Keith was laughing. I could see Boone bouncing gently up and down against the Beast suit. I was laughing. I could hear laughter around me, and then Boone turned, still in the arms of the Beast, toward me. He raised his hands and Beauty's ring sparkled.

"Cut!" he shouted. He hopped from the Beast's embrace.

Everyone clapped. Boone bowed, first left, then right and then center.

"Kristin," he said solemnly, "if you can't do at *least* that well, I clearly will have to take your part." He took off the ring and slipped it back on my finger.

"I'll never be half as good, but I have something to aim for now. I'm ready to try again. If you are."

"Better ask Keith," Boone said. "He seems to be your target."

Keith lumbered over. I realized that he must be terribly hot and uncomfortable and probably still a little damp.

This time we managed to approach the idea that Boone had of how a maiden is wooed. A few more tries and we had it down. With one more scene to go, it looked like I might get through without destroying the planet.

All I had to do was accept a bouquet of flowers.

Keith, ever so gingerly, extended his arm, offering me the bouquet. I was lying down. I rose on one elbow and reached up with my free hand, but the elbow I was balanced on slipped and I fell, pulling the flowers so hard from the Beast's hand that he lost his balance and fell onto me. We rolled toward the cameras, except that what was rolling, I suddenly realized, was just me and the Beast's head. Finally we came to a rest. I didn't want to get up or look back. Perhaps, I

85

thought, I had knocked off Keith's own head also with my graceful acceptance of the flowers. As I raised myself up and looked at everyone, all I could think of to say was, "Why didn't you yell 'Cut!'"

"And not have this on film?" Boone said. "I'll be able to blackmail you for the rest of your career. Your payments to me not to release this nationwide will ensure my old-age security. I won't need residuals. I'll be independently wealthy. I shall be known as the genius of clean household comedy. Today's performance, Kristin, will be on celluloid forever." And Boone just laughed and laughed.

I rubbed all the places on me that I'd rolled over on. "I could have been hurt," I said.

"A great director has to take risks," Boone said.

"To think that my fame will be established on film that doesn't go into a final cut," Luke, the head cameraman, said.

They were all laughing. But I hadn't heard anything from behind me — and in Boone's mood, he probably wouldn't even give Keith first aid if he was in agony. I turned around. Keith, kind Prince, was not laughing, but looking at me with sympathy and a concerned expression on his face.

"I was telling someone just the other day that I could lose my head over a girl like you," he said.

I rolled the head from its nose-forward resting

place near the edge of the set back to Keith. It had an eccentric wobble, like a huge, furry, knobby football. It came to rest at his feet, and I picked up the flowers and handed them to Keith.

"Yes, I will marry you, Beast," I said. "I will never again be able to find work in this industry, and I'd better do something practical if I am forever to make payments to the Ogre of All Time, Beast Worse than Thou."

Although a lot of time had been wasted, I think we all felt good. The laughter and the nonsense had cleared the tension from me. It even seemed that it wasn't so terribly important to have found my father. Lots of people had fathers, but not everyone had Boone and Keith and all the rest of the people on the set. A kind of family, or at least so it felt today.

But on the drive home my thoughts went to the Ahmanson. One scene more in my movie and I'd be able to catch a Saturday matinee at the Music Center.

[3] THE BLACK HOLE DISCO AND THE TALK SHOW

CLAPBOARD: ONCE UPON A GALAXY, SCENE 30

[Beauty is asleep in her elegant bedroom. Close-up of her face. She is smiling in her sleep, dreaming. Fade to the figure of the Prince, as if in a dream, misty and undefined. Beauty opens her eyes, sees the Prince and arises. She is wearing a loosely fitted metallic jumpsuit. There are jewels in her hair. She takes his hand.]

[The Control Room: The Beast watches the two figures on the screen above the control panel. As his hands move on the panel, the Prince takes Beauty's hand and they walk away. The image on the screen sharpens, becomes less dreamlike, fills the screen.]

Prince: Do you like to dance?

Beauty: *[Dreamily.]* More than anything. *[Sways to unheard music.]*

Prince: I've heard of a new place. Like to try it?

Beauty: *[Suddenly shy.]* I'd like that.

[They step into a small shining rocket, which zips off into the blackness of space. It arrives on another planet, which is shiny and bright, full of

metal and light and glass, pulsing and moving, a little showy. The Prince takes her hand and helps her from the rocket. They walk together down a corridor of flashing lights and shifting colors. They stop.]

Prince: This is it.

[They are standing before a huge black archway, above which the words "BLACK HOLE DISCO" appear written in light which fades and is rewritten over and over. They walk through the arch hand in hand. It is full of mirrors and flashing lights and flowers that look real but are enormous and moving delicately in their bouquets. There are many, many couples, all dancing. Each couple seems to be dancing to a different melody, moving at a different tempo with a different style. The range of dress is wide, from ordinary space clothing to costumes of every age and from every place. The disco is silent.]

Beauty: I don't hear any music.

Prince: They have to find out what we want to hear. What dance we prefer.

[Suddenly, as he speaks, music fills the air around them. It is a waltz. She moves into his arms and they dance through the crowd.]

Prince: This is the right dance, isn't it?

Beauty: Yes, But how did they know? I didn't know.

Prince: You must have.

[The music stops. They are still in each other's arms. Beauty pulls away, embarrassed. The music changes to wild, very rhythmic music, and they begin to dance to it. Beauty's eyes shine. The music

89

changes again, to a waltz, and they come together to dance.]

Prince: We have to leave soon.

Beauty: This is a dream, isn't it?

Prince: Perhaps it is time to wake up, Beauty.

Beauty: But I don't want to wake up.

[The music fades. In the silence the other dancers dance on around them. The Prince takes her hand and leads her out, back to the corridor of light, back to the little rocket. Silently, they enter it and it leaves.]

[Outside the Beast's castle: They are standing in a garden. The tiny rocket is behind them.]

Beauty: Am I dreaming?

Prince: Does it matter?

Beauty: *[Softly.]* No. If I have to dream to be with you, then I would dream forever.

[The Prince slowly pulls her to him and they kiss.]

[The Control Room: The Beast is watching on the screen, his hands moving rapidly over the controls. Beauty and the Prince part and the Prince turns away, back to the rocket. The Beast's hands leave the controls and he falls back against the chair, exhausted.]

Beauty: Don't go. Please don't go.

[She runs after the Prince. He turns and she reaches out her hand and touches him. The Prince shatters in an explosion of prisms that dance before her eyes, almost blinding her. Fragments of light fill the air. She covers her eyes. When she uncovers them, he is gone. The rocket is gone. She is alone in the garden. She is cold. She turns and

runs into the castle, her eyes filling with tears. As she enters the great hall, the Beast is there, waiting for her.]

Beast: What is the matter, Beauty?

Beauty: It wasn't a dream! It wasn't! I saw him. He *kissed* me.

Beast: *[Very gently.]* It was a dream, Beauty. You've been walking in your sleep.

Beauty: We were dancing. I'm wearing a beautiful . . . *[She looks down at herself. She is wearing a gown and robe, and there are no jewels in her hair, which is loose on her shoulders.]*

Beast: Tell me about the dream, Beauty. That may help.

Beauty: He had a rocket. We went to a place to dance. Everyone heard different music. We heard a waltz. *[She smiles, remembering.]*

Beast: You enjoyed that, Beauty? You like to dance?

Beauty: Oh, yes!

Beast: Would you like to dance?

[Music fills the room, the same waltz she had danced with the Prince. Beauty rises, faces the Beast. Their hands touch, barely, and slowly they waltz across the room. The music fades and they stop. Beauty's arms drop to her sides.]

Beauty: *[Tenderly.]* Don't ask me. Please.

Beast: Will you marry me, Beauty?

Beauty: *[Shaking her head, tears filling her eyes.]* I can't, dear Beast. I can't.

When we finished the morning's shooting, Keith and I ate lunch together. We did most days

91

now. His mother sent little treats for him nearly every day, since, Keith said, she was sure a growing boy withered rapidly without home cooking. The last week or so, she had sent extra — for me. I think Keith was my friend now — he had given up his lunchtime chess games anyway, and I think that's probably real friendship — but I had never thought I would acquire another family, too. Or a family. Even though I had never met them, the noon treats and Keith's talk about his brothers and sisters and parents and grandparents — all four of them — made me feel I knew them all.

He was especially quiet that noon — quiet for Keith — and we were up to dessert (I took the apples from his mother and he took the enormous piece of cheesecake which she had sent me and which I turned down reluctantly), before he said much.

"What did you think of that, Kristin?"

"Your mother sending the cheesecake? Really nice. It's just that I don't eat many sweets."

"No. The control room."

He said it so casually, as if there was a real control room, maybe one that had been in the news, that for a second I couldn't imagine what he was talking about.

"I mean," Keith went on slowly, "the Beast sits there and moves dials and controls the world — the universe, even."

I hadn't given much thought to the philosophical implications of that. To me it was just a stage set where the Beast sat and pretended to do things that couldn't be done. Because if they could be done, first, they wouldn't be impressive in the movie, and second, we wouldn't need special-effects people to make them seem to have happened. But as soon as I heard Keith's question, I knew what he meant.

"They don't work," I said.

"I know they don't work," he said. "But what if they did? What if you could do anything, fix anything, with a bunch of buttons and dials?"

"Why would anything ever go wrong?" I asked. "If you had all that power . . ." I stopped. Keith looked at me.

"I thought of that," he said. "If the Beast has the control room, how did he ever get enchanted in the first place? Or why can't he just disenchant himself?"

"It's a good question," I said. "Boone must know the answer. Did you ask him?"

"No," Keith said. "I didn't want to."

I had a faint but very deep glimmer of what he meant by that.

"I figured it out myself," Keith went on.

"And what is the answer?" I asked, sure that there was no answer.

"Somebody has a bigger control room."

I looked at Keith. He was going to be a good friend to have.

Maggie Arnold came by to be sure we were

eating properly and not planning the violent overthrow of Sound Stage 8. She beamed at us. "And what are you two talking about?" she asked, throwing little glances at the remains of our lunches. Probably counting calories or vitamins or something.

"Nothing," I said.

"Life," Keith said.

"What a *deep* conversation," she said.

"Not really," Keith said, wadding up the papers from our lunches into a rough ball. He held the ball up to his forehead, squinted in that funny way basketball players do when they're getting ready to take a free throw and tossed the wad toward an open box about twenty feet away.

He missed. The paper bounced off the edge of the box and onto the floor. Keith stood to pick up the wad, but Maggie was there first. She picked it up and dropped it into the box. "Mustn't litter," she said brightly.

"Thank you, Maggie. I won't do it again," Keith said.

As soon as Maggie was gone, I turned to Keith: "I know you want to be a doctor, Keith. Can I ask you about something medical?"

"Sure."

"What is spinal stenosis?"

"A narrowing of the passage through which the spinal cord passes. If it gets too narrow, it can cause paralysis. Did you look up dwarfs?"

"Yes. I've never known a dwarf before."

"I did too."

He'd probably read the same things I had. "Do you think Boone is going to be paralyzed? Or die? Why?"

"He probably won't be paralyzed, because they can do surgery on the spinal problems if they aren't neglected for too long. I can't imagine Boone doing anything that would hurt him. Can you?"

"No," I whispered. "I can't."

"Kristin. You were really worried about him, weren't you? I wouldn't, if I were you. I don't. He's really a smart man. He likes living. A dwarf can get sick, just like anybody else, but I don't think, except for the back problems, that it matters that he's a dwarf."

Little does he know, I thought. Of course it mattered. It mattered to Boone, I was sure.

"And 'why?' " Keith went on. "What do you mean by 'why?' Why is he a dwarf? Or why does anybody have to be a dwarf?"

I had thought I meant Why was Boone a dwarf? but the second question, Why does anybody have to be a dwarf? was the real question.

"The second."

"I don't know." He shrugged.

But I thought I knew. "It's that bigger control panel," I said.

We just smiled at each other and then went back to work.

During that afternoon it occurred to me that

Keith and I had talked. Just like Phyllis and my mother.

I had thought about asking Keith to take me to the Ahmanson, but that would have meant telling him why we were going there and I wasn't sure I was ready to share my secret with anyone. I wanted to hug my new knowledge for a while. Later, when my father and I were friends, I would tell others about him.

I should have read the play first, I knew, but there hadn't been time. I waited until the rhythm of my mother's typing had a definite momentum and then I dashed in and told her I was going to the movies. She nodded without missing a stroke and I was out of the house and off to the theater.

I saw the signboard on the corner where I got off the bus. "Ben Jonson's VOLPONE, OR THE Fox," it said. I searched for a Howard. The only one was near the bottom, in small type, in a list following "WITH." Howard Glendon. I felt a little shiver and the hair on my arms stood up, just as if I had been frightened by something. I ran up the stairs to the great quadrangle of the center. There were a lot of people there, standing around, talking, walking, and I was suddenly sure that they were all going to see *Volpone* and that I would not be able to get a ticket.

There was a ticket. Not a good one, the lady explained, but I would be able to see well enough. She didn't seem at all curious about why I was there alone, which was too bad, because I just might have told a stranger that I was going to see my father.

Inside, I got a *Playbill* and found my seat. Before I opened it I felt a need to take several deep breaths. I simply was not my usual self. The entire experience, as it was playing itself out, amazed me. I felt a split within myself, one which I hadn't known was there and one which I wasn't certain I wanted. I think of myself as a total realist and it is as such that I have been raised and have raised myself. I had thought that I wanted to solve the mystery of my existence out of curiosity and for the thrill of the chase. I thought that *knowing* was what I was really after.

But now, about to see my father, I didn't know. It was like there was this little girl in me who wanted to say "Daddy." I — or this little girl, I should say — had fantasies of going places with him, of long intimate talks, of getting advice (I, who haven't been given advice by anyone except directors in years), even of wearing especially pretty dresses for him. I was not too thrilled with this split me. I was too old to go wild over the first appearance of a father. But I couldn't get this across to this little girl inside me, who was bursting to see what her father looked like.

Split or not, there was one heart for the two of

us and it was pounding so hard that I almost couldn't sit still in our seat.

I opened the *Playbill*. And there he was. I had no doubt at all that he was my father. Blond, blue eyes. Handsome. An absolutely beautiful smile. Very young. My professional head clicked off that it was probably a very outdated photograph, but the little girl just thought he was as stunning as anyone could wish for in a father. Under the picture was a short description of the things he had acted in. It listed several plays of which I hadn't heard and several movies, one of which I had actually seen but I couldn't remember him in it. He had been in two television series, both at a time when I'd been watching *Captain Kangaroo,* and now had a continuing part in *Yesterday's Dream,* a soap opera. I'd never seen it. My mother didn't believe in soap operas, even though, I pointed out, they were a lot like romantic novels. He had also done a few off-Broadway shows and that was about as much as *Playbill* knew.

I turned my attention to the stage. Though I knew from the program that Peregrine, the Gentleman Traveller, didn't appear until the second act, I was so anxious by now that I felt a little sick to my stomach.

As soon as the curtain came up, I forgot all that. Even though I hadn't read it, the play was easy to follow. I had just settled back after Volpone's long opening speech when the servant came onstage. And with him came a dwarf. I sat up. He seemed to have a hunchback, and he pranced and capered in a way that made me very uneasy. He spoke in a high-pitched, affected voice, but I didn't hear a word he said.

All I could think of was Boone. For a minute I even forgot why I was there, my father, everything. The dwarf was, I thought, making a fool of himself. Did Boone know about this? Had he ever seen this play? The dwarf and another actor began to sing a song, dancing and gesturing. I had another thought, one so awful that the pit of my stomach hurt. Had Boone ever played this part? Had he danced and sung and giggled like this for people?

Why did my father have to be in a play with a dwarf in it?

They stopped singing and Volpone waved them away and I was so relieved as they left the stage that I wanted to clap. People came and went for the rest of the act and I lost track of what was happening as my mind buzzed and swooped from thought to thought, none of them concerning the play. When the curtain went down at the end of the first act, my hands were icy cold, because I knew that when it went up again, I was going to see my father.

As the curtain rose for the next act, I saw two men on the stage. My father, I knew at once, was the tall, slender, handsome one. The other actor spoke at length while I itched to hear my father's voice. I leaned forward in my seat.

"Yes," he said. Then "Seven weeks" and then "Not yet, sir."

It was not, I could tell, a big part.

He said more as the scene went on. He had a nice voice, I thought. A good theater voice.

And then the dwarf came back onstage and I had to divide my attention between them. My father had a few more lines, the dwarf sang two more songs and suddenly they were all gone. I slumped back in the seat. He didn't appear at all in the third act and then there was intermission. I stayed in my seat and brooded.

Maybe my father would have a larger part in the next acts.

He didn't. In fact, he mostly asked questions. He was a straight man. And, as far as I could tell, he wasn't part of the main plot.

The play ended, and as soon as the applause died down and I could make my way through the crowd, I went backstage. There were people running around moving things, actors still in costume, chatting. Several people looked at me as if they were going to say something, but I guess I looked comfortable there, because no one challenged me. I found the back exit and waited.

I was trying to decide whether I should be looking younger or older to be most inconspicuous when I saw him. He was wearing street
100

clothes and he looked smaller and paler than he had onstage. My blue eyes may have come from my mother, but I knew now who had given me my blond hair and my height.

"Mr. Glendon?" I called.

He turned with that automatic smile that actors have for situations of uncertainty. I recognized it. I have used it myself.

"Yes?" he said.

"Could I talk to you for a minute?" It was all I could think of to say.

His smile broadened and he reached for the *Playbill* I had in my hand, still turned to his picture. Before I could say anything else, he had a pen in hand and was signing his name across the picture.

"Thank you," I said, taking the program from him, "but that wasn't what I wanted . . . Could I talk to you outside? Just for a few minutes."

He hesitated, then nodded and opened the door for me.

It was crisp, a little cool outside after the warmth of backstage, and I shivered. We had come out into the area between the Ahmanson and the Mark Taper, the smaller theater, and I hurried ahead past the reflecting pool in which the white walls of the theaters waved and blurred, the blue sky a line between them. He followed me.

The expanse between the Ahmanson and the Dorothy Chandler Pavilion looked huge and

101

empty in the afternoon sunlight, the large grouping of statues in the center presiding over no one. I glanced back at my father and he looked interested and a little apprehensive.

"Over there," I said. "By the statues."

We sat.

"Young lady," he began.

"Kristin."

"Kristin, then. What was it you wanted to talk to me about?"

I hadn't actually planned this. Somehow I had imagined that he would know at once who I was and I would be spared having to put into words this very difficult truth.

"Kristin Kelley," I said. "My mother is Amanda Kelley."

His attention, which had been wandering, snapped back to me. He was silent.

"I think you're my father," I said, and added immediately, "I know you're my father."

In my head, playing the scene over and over, I had had many different reactions from him, mostly involving his throwing his arms around me, sometimes crying, sometimes not, but nothing I had thought of was as real, as wonderful, as what happened.

"Kristin," he said slowly, his eyes shining with the smallest hint of tears. "Kristin. What a beautiful name." He took my hand gently and then pulled me to him. I found myself with my face against the rough tweed of his jacket, feeling absolutely no urge to cry, which is what I had been afraid would happen. Looking up, I could see faint traces of make-up on his jaw, a smudge of it on his shirt collar, and I wanted to laugh because it was so *perfect* that my father would be an actor, would smell like an actor, of make-up and cold cream. And because I was so happy. It seemed that both my selves were in the right place at the right moment.

We were like two people in a play in the center of the big cold stage of the Music Center Plaza, looking at each other.

"Tell me," he said gently. "Did your mother tell you who I was?"

I was startled. I hadn't expected him to ask that.

I blurted it all out: the letters in my mother's files, the overheard conversation between my mother and Phyllis as I sat at the top of the stairs. He nodded just to keep me going, it seemed, whenever it sounded as though I might run down. When I finished he went back at once to the letters.

"Amanda . . . your mother . . . said . . . in the letters? That I was your father?"

"Well," I started, "I wasn't born yet, but —" I broke off. For the first time I really thought about what that letter had said. "He will never know," my mother had written, "if he has to learn it from me."

"Of course," I said. "You didn't know."

"No. I didn't know."

"Are you glad?"

He smiled. An enchanting smile. A real milk-commercial smile. "What do you think?" he said. "I have a beautiful daughter." He took my hand again. "It's just that I'm a little surprised, shocked maybe. It might take a minute or two to get used to the idea."

"How long are you going to be here?" I motioned toward the theater with my head. I started to offer to come to every matinee before I realized that I couldn't do that. I had to work.

"Another week," he said. "But I'll be around. I have a feeling that Matt is about to be written out."

I didn't realize at first that Matt was the character he played in the soap, I was so busy, so happy with the words "I'll be around."

"Then I can see you again?"

"Try to stop me. Tell me about you," he said. "What have you been doing?"

"I'm an actress," I said.

He looked hard at me. "Kristin Kelley. Of course. You were in *Not Alone at Sea*. I saw that. You were wonderful."

I blushed. Turned red like a little girl, then ducked my head. "Thank you."

"What else are you doing?"

It was a professional question, one actor to another. It made me feel proud of him and of myself, and it eased some of the tension between us. We could always talk about show business.

I told him about *Once upon a Galaxy* and Boone.

His face lit up. "That's great. He's a fine director."

"I know."

The conversation lagged from time to time, but we sat and talked as the afternoon passed. I think that anyone walking by would have known at once that we were father and daughter. He asked about my mother and I told him about her writing romances under the name Amanda Crayne.

"She doesn't act anymore, then?" he asked.

"Never." I laughed. "She hates the business, actors . . . I mean . . ."

He laughed too. "Don't apologize. I think I understand. At least she lets you do what you want. Or could she stop you?"

"I don't know," I said. I had never thought about not being allowed to act. Once I found it, nothing else that I might have done seemed to have any reality for me.

We talked about his career. He said that there was something big just around the corner. I was glad for him. He needed something better than Peregrine, the Gentleman Traveller.

I had a sudden wonderful idea. "Maybe someday we could act in something together," I said.

He swiveled toward me on the bench, a smile

lighting his face. "That would be marvelous," he said.

"Working together. Just think of it."

We sat silently for a few minutes. I was thinking of it, of being with him for days and days, seeing him all the time. He had a sort of distant, wondering expression on his face and I thought he was seeing the same pictures in his head.

He looked at his watch and I realized that he had looked at it several times before.

"Are you in a hurry?" I wanted to call him "Dad," but I couldn't get the word out.

"I'm sorry, hon." He couldn't call me "Kristin," I noticed. He hadn't called me anything yet, except, now, "hon." Maybe it was much too early for such intimacies as names and titles.

"It's okay," I lied.

"We have another performance, you know."

I had forgotten. Of course he had to leave. He had to eat something and get back to the theater in time for the evening show. I stopped feeling rejected and then there was a flurry of exchanges of phone numbers and admonitions, mostly from me. To wit: Do not talk to my mother. "She doesn't know that I know. I have to plan how to tell her."

And then he said, "That's my agent's number. Reach me through him. I'm not home very much, you know."

I knew immediately that he was living with

someone and that he didn't want me to talk to that someone.

Suddenly we were very awkward.

"I'd ask you to have dinner with me," he said, "but I'm joining someone else."

"It's all right."

"It's just that I need to think about this. To plan the right way to tell people about you."

I smiled. "I have the same problem. I think we should know each other a little better."

He was relieved. "Exactly. I may be selfish," he said, "but I don't want to share our first times together with anyone else."

That was so close to what I felt myself that I had to suppress a shiver. We were very much alike, I thought.

He left then, walking quickly away from me to disappear down the stairs at the corner. I watched him the entire way, trying to memorize the way he moved, the way his jacket fit across his shoulders, the way he bent his head as he walked forward, as if he was walking into the wind. All the things I should always have known.

All the way home on the bus, I wondered what it could have been about him that was so terrible that my mother had never wanted to marry him. When I got home she was in the kitchen humming and fixing dinner, something she rarely did, so I knew she had had a good day with her characters. I kissed her and she asked me how the movie was.

"Fine," I answered and hurried out of the kitchen before she could ask me anything about it.

I would tell her the truth very soon. Even the temporary deceptions involved in finding my father and seeing him had been a drain on me. Part of it was just seeing him, of course. But for the first time I found lies and deceptions exhausting. My mother looked especially trusting and innocent as she stirred at the stove.

But she had deceived me all these years, and that thought somehow comforted me.

By morning I still hadn't quite decided the best way to tell her, and by evening I was no closer to a decision. Her general way of handling difficulties was not to. That way they either went away or someone else handled them for her. So there was the possibility of just not telling her. But in my mind I saw myself making up the lost years with my father. She'd have to know. Why not tell her now and get it over with?

I went downstairs and heard the sound of the typewriter. That was good. She wouldn't be into her mother number, when she cooked and decided it was time to get to know her daughter, for us to share our days together. Instead, we would have Pizza Man for dinner, which would be better than another healthy omelet. Also, maybe I could just slip in the news while she was between sentences.

The typing stopped. She came out of her study. She had taken to wearing turtleneck sweaters over Levi's as a sort of writer's uniform. It also made her look about twenty-five, and I know she liked to look that way. She never wore make-up and she never got her hair done, but she did like it when people were shocked that she had a fourteen-year-old daughter. I told her I'd be happy to say I was eighteen if that would help the cause any, but she said it didn't work that way.

"Kristin, how was your day?"

The question startled me. "Fine. What makes you ask?"

"What's unusual about a mother asking her daughter how a day went?"

"Nothing. But you just don't."

"Well, I mean to. Sometimes I think of it after you've gone to sleep and I'm roaming around with my insomnia, but I've never felt you would want to be awakened and asked just then."

"That's true," I said.

"So it was a fine day."

"Fine," I said.

"Do you want Pizza Man for dinner? Or I could make you an omelet?"

"You cooked just last night, Mom."

"That's true. Well, call and order, will you?"

I went to the telephone and called and ordered the usual.

Pizza Man sometimes took ages. I never have the patience to wait. Not having patience is another one of my problems. I don't even understand how people do have patience. They just say they have patience and then they wait patiently. When I'm waiting patiently I'm thinking of nothing else except what I'm waiting patiently for. It somehow shouldn't take so much effort to wait patiently. Others get to do it with such ease.

My mother was back in her study, but the door was open, so I knew I could go in. She leaned over her desk and did not look up as I came in. I watched her go through her ritual of counting the number of pages she'd done that day. My mother is one of those people whose patience I envy. It takes her months to finish one book, but she goes at it every day. Maybe it comes with age, this patience.

"Twenty," she said, looking up at me.

"That's good," I said.

"Rosemary Daily does thirty," she said.

"Maybe she doesn't have a child."

"Six," my mother said.

"Oh, I see. Well, maybe she's just escaping from them. Maybe she has maids."

"Thank you, Kristin, you are a comfort. Rather than hire six maids, I will settle for
110

twenty pages. Why are you being so friendly today?"

"Can I sit down?"

"Uhm, something serious. Let's go in the living room. So we are sure to hear the arrival of the Pizza Man."

I followed her into the living room, and we sat on opposite ends of the deep, soft couch.

"Guess who I saw yesterday," I said. Maybe I could get into it gently.

"I hate guessing games and you know it. Who did you see yesterday?"

"Well, actually, guess what play I saw yesterday."

Now she looked hard at me. One thing about my mother, she is not dumb. Without even playing the game, she'd gotten it on the first clue.

"So," she said. "So."

I smiled at her. "*Volpone*," I said.

"I got that part. Why don't you tell me the rest?"

"You obviously know the rest. I introduced myself to my father."

"Oh, my God," she said. "Couldn't you just have watched the play, decided he was a lousy actor and not introduced yourself?"

"How do you know he's a lousy actor? He only had about ten lines."

"Guess why," she said.

"That's ridiculous," I said.

"That's the truth," she said.

111

She certainly didn't like my father. On that issue I really was not in doubt, considering the circumstances. I outwaited her now. Could she just let it drop?

"All right, Kristin. I would like to know what happened when you introduced yourself to your father. I really would like to know all about it."

I loved having her complete attention, and I told her everything about our meeting.

"You weren't disappointed?" she asked when I had finished.

"Mother, why should I be disappointed? He was so thrilled to have me for a daughter and he is so handsome and warm and, well, radiant."

"Howard, all right," she said. "Not disappointed that he's so small an actor?"

The bell rang.

"Pizza Man," she said and sprang off the couch.

We had a pleasant dinner with no further discussion of my father.

Keith and I were going to have lunch outside, still in our costumes, because we had a big scene coming up in the afternoon. I think Maggie Arnold was beginning to have hopes of a romance between us, because she did not join us for lunch. We took our lunches out into the sunshine.

Telling my mother hadn't been easy, but it had been easier than I thought it would be. Maybe
112

that was why I decided to tell Keith about my father. Or maybe it was because he talked about his family all the time and I never had much to say in response. I couldn't, even now, match him for sheer volume, but my family had the distinction of being entirely new. As big as his family was, I doubted that they had ever mislaid a father for fourteen years.

We settled in, me with my sandwich, Keith with his three or four lunches. We both drank milk, me because my mother insisted, Keith because he claimed to like it. I think he was marked by milk commercials. Keith was especially quiet, which was too bad, because I wanted him to talk. I wanted family to come up in conversation so that I could drop my father in and watch Keith's response, but if he wasn't going to talk, that would be hard.

It was hard enough having lunch with someone who was not only dressed as a dream prince, but who looked like a dream prince. I watched him from the corner of my eye. His blond hair, long for the role of the Prince, fell in silky strands over his forehead and across his cheek as he bent his head. Then, as he lifted his head, his hair fell back, revealing the strong line of his jaw and the long column of his neck, which disappeared into the aluminum-colored tunic.

I think that at that moment I was feeling at least part of what I had been pretending to feel in *Not Alone at Sea.* A sensation composed partly of a spreading warmth and partly of a distant quiver flowed through me. I could not stop looking at Keith's face, even though I knew I would be horribly embarrassed if he turned his head and saw me studying him.

That wasn't why I had asked him to have lunch with me. Or was it? My mother was always telling me that I should examine my motives because, according to her, I simply pretended to myself that I had practical, even moral, reasons for doing the things I *wanted* to do.

I had to say something about my father right now, if only to prove to myself that he was the reason for this suddenly awkward lunch.

Apparently Keith, too, had been feeling the strain, for we both spoke at once.

"My father — " I said.

"My brother — " Keith said.

"Your brother?" I pounced on his words, suddenly eager to talk about anything but my father.

Keith was too sharp for that. "Your father? You've never mentioned your father. I thought that he wasn't around," he finished delicately. Keith really was a perfect person and I tried very hard not to hold it against him.

"I've never mentioned him. You're right."

"So?"

Clearly I could not get out of it now, so I told him. Everything. Sitting on the stairs and eavesdropping on the interview and the conversation between my mother and Phyllis. I could not imagine Keith eavesdropping on anyone.

"I wish I'd been there," he said and smiled.

We were more alike than I had thought.

When I got to the part about taking the bus to the Music Center to see my father in *Volpone*, he nodded.

"I saw it. He was Peregrine, right?"

"You remember him?" I was pleased.

"You look like him, don't you?"

"I do?"

"You walk the same way." He tipped the upper half of his body forward, and I saw in my mind my father walking away from me, bent into the wind. It was an engaging way of walking for a long-lost father, but I wasn't sure it did anything for Beauty. "Like you're always thinking about the next place you're going to be."

He glanced over at me and I looked away. I had not known he had ever noticed the way I walked, much less thought about it enough to characterize it.

"You're really happy that you found him, aren't you?" Keith said. "You know, I can't imagine what it must be like not to have a mother and father, sisters and brothers."

"I'll settle for a mother and father," I said. "Sisters and brothers are part of another fantasy."

"I didn't mean that, Kristin."

I got up and moved farther from the building. We were the only people about. He followed me.

"I'm sorry. I didn't . . . I mean, they've always *been* there. I know how happy I am when one of them is gone for a while and comes home, so that what you're feeling — it must be a thousand times happier."

He had put his hand on my arm to keep me from moving away as he explained. I could feel the slight pressure and, through the thin fabric of Beauty's fancy dress, the warmth of his touch.

"It's okay, Keith," I said, turning toward him. "I understand what you mean."

"I'm happy for you. I wouldn't want to say anything that would hurt you or . . ."

We looked at each other, and so quickly that I didn't realize what was happening, he bent his head and kissed me. His lips were on mine, warm and very smooth and soft. I started to draw away and then changed my mind. There was no director to tell me how to move. Or what to feel. I felt warmth and a new, mysterious kind of comfort. Not really comfort, nothing as neutral as that, but comfort was the closest I could come to naming this new feeling.

"We're going to be late," Keith said. "I think I see people heading back to the sound stage."

I looked at him, trying to decide if that was regret in his voice. I thought I could hear, as the doors to the building opened and closed, faint sounds of our fantasy life being cranked back into existence. I started gathering the remains of our lunches, trying to pretend as if nothing out of the ordinary had happened. As if Kristin Kelley got kissed every day. By a prince.

Later that afternoon, when we had finished shooting, Boone asked me if I'd like to stay and watch some special effects with him, and I agreed. We went into the little theater. The lights went out and I heard the whirring of a projector.

The screen popped out with light. And more light. Colors and shapes. A montage of special effects. We saw Beauty's father's spaceship being buffeted by the storm. The rosebushes growing, budding, flowering. A spaceship beginning as a shimmer in the desert air and collecting into a needle of silver and light.

When the lights went up again, Boone turned to me: "What did you think of that, Kristin?"

I didn't know what to say. Seen like this, without people or words or action, the special effects had been interesting but not moving. My natural impulse, which has always been to say exactly what I thought, was for the first time tempered by a desire to please. I wanted more than anything not to lose whatever respect Boone had for me.

"Interesting," I said.

"Only interesting?"

"Amazing?" I offered tentatively, hoping it would serve.

"Also ingenious? Technically brilliant?"

I swiveled in the chair so that I could look at him. "Boone, are you teasing me?"

"Maybe a little." He was laughing now.

"I thought you said they were magicians, the special-effects men."

"I did. And they are. But before they can do anything, someone has to want something special from them, some illusion that can't be created on a set."

We walked slowly out of the building, past the security guard at the door and into the parking lot. Boone had offered to drive me home again.

"Are you saying that *writers* are the magicians?"

"I am. And they are." He opened the car door, waited until I was inside and then closed the door. That had embarrassed me the first time he did it, but now I enjoyed it. It made me feel very special.

"So special-effects people are magicians. And writers are magicians."

"And the *real* magicians are," he said, leaning toward me and dropping his voice to a whisper, "you" — he pointed at me — "and me" — he pointed at himself.

"You maybe. But me?"

He laughed. "You especially. You're an

actress, Kristin. Did you know that? Really know it?''

I nodded.

"The real magic is taking somebody else's words, listening to somebody else's instructions and then making a character so real that people believe in her.''

"Do I do that?" I whispered.

"You fooled me," he said briskly. "And if you can fool me, you can fool anybody.''

The soft time was over, the little glimpse of the Boone behind the wise eyes.

"Oh, you," I said. "Anybody can fool you.''

"In short, you mean I am gullible?" He started to laugh.

I caught on right away. "Just short of a proper caution.''

"Short of funds, too.''

"Is that why we're shorthanded?''

"I'll make short work of you, my child.''

"Are we taking a shortcut?''

"I *am* a shortcut!''

"Don't sell me short, Boone.''

"You may call me Boo, for short," he cried.

I was laughing now and so was Boone. "I'm short of breath," I said. "Please stop . . .''

" — short.''

By the time I got home, I thought of "don't be short with me" and "the long and the short of it" and "to make a long story short.''

We were in front of my house. I hopped out quickly, before he could get out and come around to open the door. I went to the window on the driver's side. "Thank you, Boone, for showing me the special effects."

"There's another one," he said. "But you can't see it yet."

I wanted to ask him what it was, but the light went on over the front door and I knew my mother had seen us drive up.

"Go inside, Kristin. I'll see you tomorrow." It was his director's voice and I obeyed. But I wondered for a long time what special effect I hadn't seen, that I couldn't see, yet.

After that day at the Ahmanson, I had expected to hear from my father right away, the next day, but I didn't. And not the day after that, either. We did have a problem, since I couldn't really call him and he couldn't really call me, but somehow I had expected him to find a way around that.

Almost a week went by. At home I jumped every time the phone rang. He was an actor. He could call and be someone else and my mother would never know. Or I could call him and be . . . who? Did he have a sister, a mother, aunts? I didn't know anything about my father, not even enough to pretend.

It all began to seem more and more like a dream to me. I hadn't had a father for all of my fourteen years. What made me think I could have one now? I was hurt, rejected, angry, morose, touchy. Everyone noticed. Even my mother asked me what was wrong, although she must have known. "Nothing," I snapped.

Boone was a little more direct. I was to pay attention or else. I was too distracted even to argue with him or to demand to know what "else" was, as I would normally have done. He looked worried and I caught him looking at me several times, glancing away when I saw him. I imagined he was gentler with me, but that was probably an illusion.

CLAPBOARD: ONCE UPON A GALAXY, SCENE 32

[The main room of the castle: Beauty is looking from a window. The Beast enters.]

Beast: And what are you thinking, Beauty?

Beauty: *[Slowly.]* Of my little brother. And my sister. I wonder if they miss me.

Beast: I would miss you if you were gone, so I am sure they do too.

Beauty: And my father. Is he well?

Beast: He is well.

Beauty: But I would like to see them for myself. Talk to them. *[Crosses to the Beast's side.]* Dear Beast, if you knew how lonely I am.

Beast: I know how lonely it can be here.

Beauty: If I could only see them for a little while.

Beast: Would you be happy then?

Beauty: Oh, yes!

Beast: Would you come back to . . . this place?

121

Beauty: Do you mean would I come back to you? Of course I would. I have promised I would stay with you.

Beast: You may leave if you wish. You know that. *[Hands her a ring.]* Take this with you. Stay no longer than four weeks.

Beauty: And if I do not return?

Beast: Why, I would die . . . of loneliness. The ring will bring you back. Just twist it on your finger and you will be here, just in this spot. There are boxes of gifts in your room to take back with you. Stand by them now and I will send you back to your family.

Beauty: *[Turns excitedly to leave and then turns back to the Beast.]* There are boxes there already? Did you know, then, that I would wish to leave today?

Beast: *[Turns his back on her.]* I knew. So go, Beauty. Go now.

[Beauty leaves, stopping again and again to look at the figure of the Beast, who is now standing where she stood, looking from the window.]

As soon as I heard Boone's "Cut!" I walked off the set. And there, standing by Maggie Arnold, was my father. What a simple solution. How clever of him to think of that.

"Kristin?"

"Dad?" As simply as that, we got past that barrier.

"Is there somewhere we could talk?"

"We can talk in here." I took his hand and led him toward my dressing room. What I really wanted to do was dance and shout and drag him out for everyone to see.

"Nice," he said, looking around.

"I'm so glad you came," I said. "I was so worried."

"Worried?" He looked surprised.

Maybe fathers didn't have the same sense of time as daughters. "It's been a week." I didn't want to make him mad at me.

"I was busy," he said. "The play. The soap. And there never seemed to be the right time to call."

"Me too," I said. I was smiling so hard my face ached. "But you're here."

"Did you tell your mother?" he asked.

"Yes."

"What did she say?"

"Not much."

"Is it all right that you're seeing me?"

"My mother seems to think it's my business now."

"You looked good." He nodded toward the set.

"You saw me?" I was glad I hadn't known he was there watching. I usually don't mind if people watch — my mother, Phyllis — but somehow I believe that if I had known he was there, I would have frozen, stumbled, forgotten my lines.

"Remember what you said at the Ahmanson about our working together?"

I nodded. He's arranged something so that we can work together, I thought.

"Because I've had this great idea for the two of us!"

"The two of us," I prompted.

"A script idea. A movie. Television. I'm not sure. But listen to this. It's a natural. A father and daughter who don't know the other exists.

"How they find each other," he was going on. "What it does to their separate lives." He looked at me and smiled.

"It sounds great," I said.

"Actually," he said, "I'm about half finished with the script. With the publicity we could get, it would be a sensation."

"Publicity?" I repeated foolishly.

"You know. How you and I found each other."

"Oh. Now?"

He dismissed "now" with a wave. "Not yet. We have to wait until the right moment. If we do it too soon, people will forget. Too late and it's just another publicity stunt."

We couldn't have that, I thought. Use up a perfectly good reunion because our timing was bad.

"Boone's a big director. It's lucky you got this part."

"I know that," I said. I was going to say some-

thing about it not being all luck, but he went on talking: "How do you get along with him?"

It almost sounded like an interview. People always wonder what it was like, working with Boone.

"Fine, we get along fine," I said.

"I mean, does he like you?"

Did Boone like me? No interviewer had asked that. "I think he does," I said slowly. "I like him."

My father sank down on the little daybed that I was supposed to use for naps. "That's great, hon. What we'll need, Kristin, is this: If I finish the script, would you show it to Boone? For us? It would be a wonderful break for both of us."

"Of course," I said, afraid that my voice was going to break as I spoke. It immediately felt like it would be an awkward thing to do, but of course I would show the script to Boone. What else could I do?

He jumped up. "I've got to run. But I'll get back to you with a script to show him as soon as I can."

At the door he turned and took my hand. His hand was warm and soft. "In case you need to talk to me, call me at my agent's. I'm so glad you had this idea, Kristin."

And he was gone.

I undressed slowly, creaming off the make-up that made me beautiful for the camera. I

practiced my smile, the one that was so much like my father's. We would work together, I thought. I would see him every day. We would get to know each other. I would find out if he had a sister, a mother and father, aunts and uncles. Did he play games? Did he like to swim?

I stopped with my hand in mid-air as the thought came to me: I could have more grandparents. Why hadn't I asked him if his parents were still living? But even as I finished dressing in my street clothes, I had decided that he had a mother who lived in Florida. My grandmother took shape in my mind. She was tall and white-haired and elegant. She moved into one of the compartments of my mind, right next to the fading image of the stunt man. She was going to be so happy to learn that she had a granddaughter. I wondered if I should suggest to my father that he put that in the script or if he would think of it by himself.

At home that night my mother returned to the subject of my father: "Any word from your father?"

"Does it show? He came to the set today. He's writing a script for both of us to be in. Him and me."

Pure dismay crossed her face. Then she sighed deeply. "For the two of you?"

"Yes. He said he loves my work."

"And he knows you're up for an Emmy?"

"Yes, he even knows that."

"At least he's kept up with *Variety*."

"Mother, would you be jealous if I appeared in a play with Daddy and by Daddy?"

"I'd be sick," she said. "But I don't pick your scripts. You and your agent do. Have you seen it, the actual play?"

"He's just finishing it now," I said.

I saw her visibly relax. "Okay," she said.

"What's okay?"

"You act in it after he's finished it. He won't."

"How do you know he won't?" I almost shouted.

"He was just finishing a play when I first knew him."

"So?"

"So, he didn't and he won't."

"Well, Mother, you're going to be wrong this time."

"We'll see," she said.

THE LAST HOUR TALK SHOW

I was dressed in a very modest pink outfit and ready long before Boone was expected. I hovered over my mother as if I wanted her to tie a ribbon in my hair. She had not wanted to come to the taping, feeling that it would ruin *The Last Hour Talk Show* for her. She did not want to believe, she said, that all those talk shows were done earlier in the day, because they would no longer feel right to her as the perfect programs for her late-night moods. My mother could go

from *The Tonight Show* through *The Tomorrow Show* and into *The Today Show* without more than a nod-off for two or so hours. She claimed that what was missing from her life was a *Yesterday Show*. She refused to read newspapers.

Not one for ribbons, she did at least stop and say that I looked fine for the show. She said that I looked fourteen, which would be so startling in anyone on television that I would win the nation's heart. To her all other teen actresses were made to look twenty-one.

"Do you think he'll talk to me a whole lot or to Boone more, maybe? I hope he talks to Boone a lot."

"It's a pleasure to see you nervous like this, Kristin. It's the way people who care about their schoolwork have been known to feel before exams."

"Did you?"

"No, I never cared about my schoolwork."

"What made you nervous, then?"

"Nothing," she said.

I believed her. I'm sure that it's genetically determined and that I'll find my father probably cared about his schoolwork or where would I have so missed out on steel nerves?

Suddenly I saw that my mother had that look in her eyes that could ignite a Las Vegas marquee ablaze with the words, "THIS IS SERIOUS, KRISTIN."

She began: "I do not in general mind if people

are realistic or not. In general that's often just as well all around. However, in this instance I feel a motherly duty to shove you toward reality. You are going on Sonny Johnson's show as bait to get Adam Michael Boone on. Try to remember that. He has never done anything like this."

"Why is Boone doing it, then, if not for publicity?"

Blues to blues. "I believe it is because he likes you, Kristin. This is not a totally novel experience for you, I hope?"

When my mother really talks to me, I go totally off balance.

"Who else likes me?" I asked.

"I do," she said, but the doorbell rang before she could go on.

She went to the door. It was Boone. "Mrs. Kelley, good to see you." He bowed.

"Would you like to come in?"

Boone checked his watch. "No, I think we must be going. Some other time, perhaps?"

"I'd love it." My mother smiled at him, and you could see that the effect of such stunning brightness, rarely shone on anyone, was not lost on him. My mother, though little is made of it by her, could play Beauty in any sequel in which Beauty grows up.

We drove to Burbank and I asked questions about going on location the following week. "Hard, hard work, barren, barren desert. To be transformed into THE PLANET OF THE

129

BEAST. Not too much shooting, not too many scenes. But *reality*."

Both of them, on one day, into reality.

"Are you nervous about going on television live like this?" Boone asked.

"No," I lied.

"Why do you lie so much, Kristin?"

"What makes you think I'm lying?"

"You are, aren't you?"

"No. Certainly not."

"Well, in that case the conversation ends here. I myself am not nervous, but miserable. But when it is over we will go someplace I like and have some fun."

"Where?"

"Old Hollywood location. You'll see."

"Boone . . ."

He smiled over at me. Guess he knew from the tone of my voice what I had been about to say.

"You are, aren't you?" he said.

"Very. I mean, Sonny Johnson is the top of the line."

"True," Boone said. "True."

"Well, now that I've admitted I'm nervous, aren't you going to tell me how to get over it?"

"Oh, you can't get over it. Nothing short of deep hypnosis would get you over it, and that would leave you too sleepy to get to the studio."

"Why did you bring it up, then?"

"To draw us closer together, my Beauty. I brought it up to reassure myself that you are human like the rest of the actors and actresses I've known."

"Do I pass?"

"Yes. You, me and everybody else. All the same. We all pass."

At Burbank we were directed around to the stage entrance for *The Last Hour Talk Show*. A man met us at the door and introduced himself, but I did not catch his name. He led us to a backstage room where we would work with the make-up artist and then watch the show on monitors until we went on. We would not speak with Johnson himself until we were on the air. There was an air of easy, practiced efficiency all about us, and we just went where we were led and waited patiently. Finally the man who had met us came in, said, "Follow me," and took us to the curtain entrance Sonny always emerges from. We could hear the introductions as we stood there.

Then we were on. Sonny Johnson had introduced me, saying that I was "already establishing a name for herself as a serious American actress." I got so wrapped up in repeating that to myself that I barely heard all he said about Boone, but I did hear the words "reclusive genius, whom we are so glad to have here."

And there we were, walking across the stage over to the familiar desk and guest seats of *The Last Hour Talk Show*. My mother has not let me taste champagne yet — beer, yes, but champagne not yet, she says — but I suspect that

131

walking toward that desk to shake hands with Sonny Johnson is what it is like to have successfully drunk just the right amount of champagne.

"It's indeed a pleasure to have you here, Adam Michael Boone . . . Mr. Boone. What shall I call you?"

"Boone is fine," Boone said. He appeared absolutely at ease. You'd think it was his set, his crew and his interview.

Johnson smiled. From this close, and even with the lights, the audience and my being nervous, I felt he was even nicer than I'd always believed. For an instant I wondered how I would have felt if instead of it being Howard Glendon in Phyllis's file, it had been a big star like Sonny Johnson. I didn't like myself for that thought; I'd just found the man, after all, and already saw that he was the perfect father for me. Just me wanting that old dog Fame, I guess. Sonny Johnson for a father.

He was totally enchanted with Boone, that was obvious.

JOHNSON: Everybody in the business knows Adam Michael Boone doesn't give interviews or do publicity for movies, etcetera. I'm delighted to have you here. I admit to having seen your second movie, *Dull Stars,* three times, so you know I liked it. But what made you decide to accept our invitation?

BOONE: *(laughing)* I always thought I'd botched that one. It was my first attempt at trying to portray Middle American families living out their lives without advantage of fame, fortuitous events or rioting in the streets. I thought it dull, I'm afraid.

JOHNSON: No, you pulled it off. It'll be around a long time, a long time. Did you see it, Kristin?

KRISTIN: No, I didn't.

JOHNSON: Of course, your mother would have probably had to carry you to the theater in a bassinet, but we won't get into the how-long-agos-was-it. Boone, you haven't answered my question.

BOONE: Why I came? I think there comes a time to talk. I thought I'd do my first time when Kristin did hers. I'll give it this one shot.

JOHNSON: Do you like to do this, Kristin? Be on a talk show?

KRISTIN: I love it. I used to have the fantasy of being on your show.

JOHNSON: Is that really true? Don't say it just because you know I want to hear it and might invite you back again sometime if you say the right thing. Now, as I said, is that really true?

KRISTIN: It would be true even if you weren't twisting my arm.

BOONE: Speaks up, doesn't she?

JOHNSON: Is she hard to work with?

BOONE: Yes, but all actors are.

JOHNSON: Why do you say that?

BOONE: The whole thing's hard — getting people to be other people than who they really are when it's hard enough just to be whoever it is you really are yourself.

JOHNSON: I see what you mean. When did you first decide to act or direct or write? You do them all.

BOONE: The answer's sort of strange. For a long time I didn't have a high opinion of myself. *(Some of the audience start to laugh.)*

JOHNSON: That's a very *low* form of humor, but one I'll bet you're familiar with.

BOONE: I have a collection of ten mil' on puns and jokes involving the words "little," "short," "pint-size," "low" and so on. Some of them are sort of funny, I guess. I collected them in self-defense.

JOHNSON: Please, Boone. Go on. You were talking about coming to acting.

BOONE: Yes, well. As I said, I felt I had some shortcomings —

JOHNSON: *(laughing)* Now, if you're going to keep that up —

BOONE: No, I won't. You can understand how I felt when I got into high school. I had no goal for myself. My family had dissuaded me from trying to become a pilot when I was in that phase, a phys-ed instructor the summer I went through that, and they thought the police department unlikely when I went through that phase. So there I was, going along, studying, reading (which, thank God, sweetened all my childhood as now it does my life), carousing already far beyond a high school level, when one day one of those little things happened which change a person's sense of self.

(Boone really seemed to be enjoying Johnson a lot. I might as well not have been there, except that it was so interesting. I didn't have any one thing that had changed my life.)

BOONE: It was in science class, and the teacher had asked about the wiring and the currents and switches in a machine he'd diagrammed on the board. It was sort of, How could this be made to light up if all the following conditions existed, etcetera? And nobody could get the answer. But I had it, and the teacher wanted to go on and either didn't see my hand raised or just figured that I, too, would give the wrong answer. I shouted and jumped up and down, calling more attention to myself than I had ever voluntarily done. I kept yelling, "But I know, let me tell." It was probably ludicrous to watch, but the teacher stopped to humor me and said, "All right, Adam, how is it done?"

I explained it. And I could just see the look of respect on his face and feel it in the kids around me. And I knew then that I was going to be able to do things because of my mind that other people couldn't do. It was a turning point. Until that day I really think I mostly noticed what other people had that I didn't, rather than what I had that they didn't.

Until then I was very into bodies — theirs

135

and mine. So much energy into that. When I switched the energy from body to mind, something happened to me. I could take on any body I wanted and be it — for a while. I acted whatever roles I could get, and once I started it was all I wanted — except later, when I wanted to be a priest.

JOHNSON: Had you started acting yet?

BOONE: No, but after that day I did. I believed I could create landscapes with my mind and fit right into them.

JOHNSON: I think I know what you mean. I felt that way about magic. Even doing card tricks, I felt like I was creating a special space to be in for a limited time.

KRISTIN: You had time limits?

JOHNSON: Oh, yes. Because I knew that illusions couldn't last indefinitely even when I made them real.

BOONE: That's true. Isn't all writing, directing, acting, a way of saying, "Come here, come into my magic tent for a while, and while you're here I'll show you —"

JOHNSON: What do you think, Kristin?

KRISTIN: Yes. In Boone's new movie I go dancing with the Prince at the Black Hole Disco, and while I'm in that time-space I can hear any tune I want.

JOHNSON: I detect a movie plug entering our time-space. Kristin, did you want to act when you were younger?

KRISTIN: I always wanted to act. Would do anything to get a role I wanted.

JOHNSON: Why do you think you want to do
that?

KRISTIN: Deep down under, I think it's because
it makes me feel important.

JOHNSON: Out of the mouths of babes. What do
you say to that, Boone?

BOONE: It never hurt anyone to feel important.

JOHNSON: With that we turn to some important
news from one of our sponsors.

(During the commercial, Johnson and Boone
talked baseball statistics. While they talked I
thought of how funny it felt to be telling the truth
right from the top of my head, just straight out. It
was physically tingling. It did occur to me not to
panic over my behavior. I could lie the next day
— tell any story I wanted, as I had always done.
But there did seem to be something unique about
the truth. Not a good thing or a bad thing or
anything like that. Nothing moral. Just unique.
A sensation of I'll-just-tell-the-truth-and-if-they-
don't-like-me-they-don't-like-me.

The signal came on and we were back on the
air.)

JOHNSON: What were you thinking about, Kristin, so seriously there?

KRISTIN: About lying.

JOHNSON: Oh, go right ahead and lie. Say anything you want. Tell a big one. There's nothing
that hasn't been said by someone sitting there.

KRISTIN: I don't have a particular lie I want to tell.

JOHNSON: Wait until you're older. It'll come more naturally.

BOONE: Maybe it won't. Maybe she'll stay clean. Let's not discourage her.

JOHNSON: We don't have a lot of time left, Boone, but you mentioned that you studied for the priesthood.

BOONE: Yes, I did.

JOHNSON: Despite your obvious gifts for the theater?

BOONE: Well, I believe everything we are given is a gift.

JOHNSON: *(after hesitation)* Even your, uh, "condition"?

BOONE: My dwarfism. Yes. Even that. That, you might say, was a birthday present. You have to remember that sometimes you get a gift and you can't imagine why you got that particular item.

JOHNSON: *(laughing, but gently)* No one has ever said anything quite like that on this show before.

There was actually about five seconds of silence.

JOHNSON: Feeling the way you do, what made you decide to stop studying for the priesthood? The call of acting?

BOONE: No, women.

JOHNSON: Hah, just like the rest of us.

BOONE: Yes, just like the rest of you — although I hadn't realized you'd studied to be a priest.

JOHNSON: *(laughing)* No, I didn't mean that. Just that a lot of us have changed plans for women. What kind of women do you find most appealing?

BOONE: Beautiful, brilliant and short.

JOHNSON: Kristin, I know you're only fourteen, but if you were eighteen, would you want to date your director?

KRISTIN: I don't know. He's very demanding and a perfectionist. I'm not at all sure he'd want to date me.

JOHNSON: *(teasingly)* Well, Boone?

BOONE: Depends on whether or not she wins the Emmy.

JOHNSON: We'll be right back with Kristin and Boone, after this special word from our sponsors.

When we were back on the air again, Johnson changed the subject.

JOHNSON: What do you do for relaxation, Boone?

BOONE: I read, listen to music, play bridge.

JOHNSON: And you, Kristin?

KRISTIN: I'm too young to relax. My mother says it won't work into my schedule until I'm nineteen. Then it will be too late to do me any harm.

JOHNSON: Well, parents of America, do you all hear that? I did not say that, my guest did.

KRISTIN: Not even your guest. Her mother.

JOHNSON: That clarifies the issue. We'll take another little break now.

From the monitor I heard, "Here's a word about tomorrow's guests," and I looked at my watch and whispered to Boone, "I think it's over." And when the camera did come back, Johnson thanked us and talked about the next night's guests.

When the taping was finished, he shook hands with Boone, kissed me on the cheek and wished me luck on the Emmy. And then we were over and out.

We were zooming along toward Hollywood from Burbank pretty much in silence when I asked the question on my mind: "Would you date me if I were a grownup?"

Boone responded angrily, "That's a dumb question, Kristin."

I was hurt. "Well, if you think it's dumb, forget it," I said. "I wouldn't have mentioned it if Johnson hadn't brought it up."

"It's over both our heads, Kristin, let's drop it. Okay?"

"Where are we going?" I asked, the other issue falling away from us till it was way behind on the freeway.

"To Hollywood, my favorite part of Los Angeles. And to my favorite ice cream spa."

"Now, that sounds good," I said.

We parked at a meter on Hollywood

Boulevard. "It's a few blocks down," Boone said, "but I love to walk on this street."

We walked at Boone's pace, which I am getting better and better at making my own rather than walking two feet ahead of him and then backing up, which makes me feel awkward and makes him feel I don't know how but it can't be good. It was Hollywood and Las Palmas, ten at night. I became aware of the people around me. There was nobody within sight who would ever be walking in Santa Monica.

There were kids who zipped past on roller skates and wearing stereo earphones and who were really off in space at our Black Hole Disco as far as I could see. There were hustlers and cruisers, addicts and winos. People fatter than you usually see and older and emptier than you usually see. And vacant people who could bump into Boone and not even notice him. Where were the tourists? I wondered, but I could not spy out any. The street we walked on seemed given over to people who anywhere else might have hesitated to walk on the street. No one here was outnumbered by anyone else.

"Boone, are you noticing the people?"

"Yes."

"Do we belong?"

"I belong. You're just along for the ride."

"Like in one of Beauty's dreams?"

"I'm glad you see it that way. Some might say nightmare."

141

I knew what he meant. It wasn't your average group of Americans out for the evening air. But I liked it. I got caught up into whatever special effect was holding Hollywood Boulevard together this way. There had to be danger lurking. All the iron gratings on the stores proclaimed that if theft might be practiced, it would be, and the extra number of patrolling police cars came to one's attention. But on the whole I still felt a sense of community among these people, who had all seemed to agree to be on the street together, all hands off, everybody do his own thing, ignore any passersby who just strolled in. Let them stroll out. This is our street tonight.

"Let me take you away from all this," Boone said, directing me toward Swensen's.

"Oh, great," I responded.

"Table?" the waitress asked when we went in.

"Please," Boone said.

She led us to a table that looked out onto the Boulevard, and I felt like we'd been set onto an island just offshore from where the action was.

"What do you want, Kristin?" Boone said.

"Can I have a banana split?"

"As many as you want. The camera can always change angles if you gain twenty pounds tonight."

"Made up your minds?" the waitress asked.

"Two banana splits, please."

"Anything to drink?"

"Maybe later for me," Boone said. "Kristin?"

"Nothing for me." I started to giggle.

"What's so funny?" he asked.

"It feels like we're on a date. The way we just ordered and you so polite to me. The whole thing."

He laughed. "Well, if my charm overwhelms the waitress and she tries to take me away from you, I'll tell her you're the one of us with the money. Otherwise I wouldn't date you."

She brought the banana splits. Banana splits are truly works of art. They are physically beautiful. If the whipped cream is done right, and it was on these, then the colors of vanilla, chocolate and strawberry blend with the toppings of chocolate, marshmallow and pineapple and could honor a Matisse anytime. And they had it in the right dish, the boat, rather than in a parfait glass with one scoop on top of another.

"Wow!" I said.

"I agree," Boone said.

We ate companionably.

Then I asked him: "You really hated the talk show, didn't you?"

"Yeah, I did."

"You did it just for me, didn't you?"

He nodded. "You've grown on me."

I looked up from my remaining mishmash of melting split and looked into his eyes. There's so much of Boone that is irregular that one might want to stare at just to see how it is shaped, where it fits together with whatever it fits together with, but oddly enough it was his eyes I could never look into long enough. I had never felt this about anyone before. Boone's eyes are blue, which everyone knows and sees. But just then as I looked into them I thought that they contained the universe. I can never imagine the number of stars I hear about. I cannot truly visualize a black hole. Looking into Boone's eyes, I thought he saw it all. If I could look deeply enough, patiently enough, I, too, could understand everything. But I couldn't.

I didn't have the courage to look hard enough. What would I be if I had the knowledge Boone appeared to have? Who would I be? It would be scary to be Boone. He was a crippled dwarf and maybe was becoming more crippled every day. But in the light and changing blueness of his eyes — for the blue in his eyes moves and changes — he is totally whole. And that is scary, though I don't know why.

"Boone, I'm sorry you did it if you hate it so much. You do tell the truth, though, I think, don't you?"

"Mostly."

"Then why is it so awful?"

"Whenever I did get interviewed anywhere, I felt like I was some kind of dwarf or something. It's a very uncomfortable feeling."

"Johnson didn't make much out of it."

"Out of *it*," he said. "Ah, you too, then, think I'm a dwarf or something. Is my assumption correct?"

I laughed. "Well, I do think it, I'll admit. But I'm not out of high school yet, so maybe I'm wrong."

He laughed. "The point of it, Kristin, is that everybody who watches me on that talk show sees a dwarf and everybody pretends he doesn't see a dwarf. I would have been the best emperor in the world for 'The Emperor's New Clothes.' People would have denied even seeing the emperor."

"What do you want people to do?"

Boone looked sad. "Basically, leave me alone and never ask me questions, but if I'm there already they might as well stop acting like I'm Kirk Douglas and asking me which leading lady have I most enjoyed playing with."

"You sound like you want them to ask you how it feels to be a dwarf."

"If they did, I'd say 'low.' "

His eyes were smiling now, and I suddenly felt on safe territory to ask a lot of the questions he might have been asked.

"What if they asked you, 'Did being a dwarf hinder your getting to be a director?' "

"Then I'd say, 'No, from where I started it was just a short climb to the top.' "

I laughed.

Boone said, "One always needs a straight man. It is the dream of every artist to carry a straight man around with him. Of course I always thought mine would be smaller than you are, and I wasn't prepared for a female straight man, but an artist takes what is sent by the gods. Go on, ask me anything. Think of the questions that a talk-show host might ask if he was not wholeheartedly trying to slouch down to my height."

"Does it bother you, sitting on this box for this interview?"

"Frankly, I'd feel sillier on an elephant."

"Mr. Boone, did you ever wish you'd never been born?"

"Once, when I didn't make the U.S. Olympic men's basketball team."

"How did your parents feel about having you as a baby?"

"Well, they had six more after me."

"Really?"

"Yes."

"And they were all — "

"Big. All of them."

"That's a large family. Do you think your parents were compensating, proving that they could have normal children?"

"They always told me that they had so many because they wanted another one like me."

I cracked up at that one. "Do I get the job?"

"Well, you would, Kristin, except that I want

146

a midget so I can just carry this person with me in my pocket."

"I do the best I can, boss."

"Those were good questions, Kristin. And nobody asks them."

I was finished with my banana split. He was still eating his, going at it very meticulously, almost as though setting up for a scene, each spoonful exactly right.

"Want another banana split?" he asked.

I seriously considered it but fought the impulse. "No, thank you."

"What's the other question I see in the back of your head?" he asked.

"It's not for stage use."

"Fair enough. I will take it seriously."

"Do you believe in God or evolution?"

"Some of both," he answered quite seriously.

"Which the most?"

"God, I think," he said.

"But isn't it better, like easier, to think that evolution made you the way you are rather than a knowing God?"

"Am I so bad, then, Kristin?"

I saw the horror of my question like a springing, flooding of space in my brain.

I reached out and took his small hand. "Oh, no, Boone, no." It was the first time I had ever touched him, and it felt strange.

"I prefer to think that it was God's choice that I am this way."

"You studied a lot about God, didn't you?"

"I did."

"So you know a lot." I had never heard much about God around my house.

He laughed. "It doesn't seem to work out that way. I only know one thing."

"What?"

"That God can give you strength, courage. If you pray for strength and courage, you get it. It's the only thing I've found that I could get through prayer."

"Why is that, Boone? That you can pray for one thing and not another?"

"I don't know. It's taken me all my life to find out this much."

I nodded. "Don't you get angry at God, you know, for things . . ."

He understood what I meant. "Frequently," he answered, and that set us both off to giggling. The waitress brought us our check and there we sat, giggling.

"You two sure know how to go through banana splits," she said.

"Let's go," Boone said in a stage whisper. "We've got to get all the way over to Baskin Robbins before they close."

He paid and we went into the streets again.

[4] FATHERS

Days went by and I didn't hear from my father again. I had found a place where I could occasionally watch a television set during breaks, and twice I had managed to be there at the right time to see *Yesterday's Dream*. My father was probably right about Matt, his character, being written out. He seemed to be both terminally ill and not very interesting. Between Matt and Peregrine, I figured he was too busy to get in touch with me or to do much writing on the script. But *Volpone* would be closing soon, and I knew that then we would start our long conversations about our lives so that he would have material for the script.

I was so sure of this that when Maggie Arnold said one day, "Kristin, you've got a call," I never thought of my father.

But it was my father on the phone. "I'd like to see you, Kristin," he said.

I had been without a father for so long, had found him so recently, that for a minute I could not fit this voice, this person, into my life. I thought about him a lot, every day, but it seemed that when I was not thinking of him, he was not

149

yet a firm enough part of my life to be instantly recalled.

"I'd like to see you too, Dad."

"Tomorrow?"

"I'm working," I said.

"Lunch?" he suggested. "I can't manage dinner for another week."

If he was free for lunch, Matt must be gone, I realized. "Lunch would be fine. I'll check, but I think it's okay."

"I'll pick you up. What time?"

"Noon."

"At noon. By the studio gate on Pico. Do you like Italian food?"

"Love it," I said.

The next day I was waiting by the gate a little before noon, having arranged to go, taken off my make-up and put on my street clothes in about three and a half minutes.

At twelve-thirty my father drove up and honked. I had to push trash off the seat as I hopped in the car. It was an old black VW squareback. I leaned over and kissed him on the cheek, and he turned his head, looking surprised. I kept forgetting that he wasn't any more used to having a daughter than I was to having a father.

"My car's in the shop," he said. "I hope this one won't embarrass a big star like you." He smiled.

"I usually take the bus."

"Doesn't your mother drive?"

150

"Only when she has to." I didn't want to talk about my mother. I wanted to talk about us.

We pulled up in front of an Italian restaurant named Anna's. My mother and father both liked Italian food, but that — and a baby — had apparently not been enough of a foundation for marriage.

The maitre d' knew my father. They called each other "Andy" and "Howard." Apparently they had arranged that we would have a table in the farthest room, which was the quietest part of the busy restaurant.

We sat in one of the red booths and I noticed that my father was carrying a folder, which he put on the table between us. He wanted to order pizza, but I explained that I had to be back at one-thirty sharp, so we both ordered salads, which I expected would be quick to come. I kept looking at the folder, trying to figure out what could be in it. I thought of pictures of my mother and father when they were young, when they were both acting. I never thought of the script. After all, he still didn't know my half of the story.

But it was the script. He pushed it across the table to me.

"I finished it," he said. "The script," he added, at the look of surprise on my face.

"You finished it? But how?"

"Hard work," he said, smiling. "Nights and nights."

That hadn't been what I meant at all, but

thinking of it, I knew he must have worked hard to have done it in such a short time with the other things he had to do. I started to open the folder and he put his hand over mine.

"Don't read it now. Wait until you can read it all at once. I think it's better that way."

Obediently, I closed the folder, but the words inside seemed to burn through the paper, I wanted to see them so badly.

The salads came and we started to eat. At least, my father started to eat. The combination of the script right there in front of me and the excitement of the first meal I had ever had with my own father took all my appetite away, and I pushed pieces of lettuce around absently. I really wanted to talk.

"I'm out of *Yesterday's Dream*," he said finally. "The fools killed off Matt. I told them it was a mistake."

"But he was sick," I blurted out. "Fatally ill." That was how it had been described in one of the episodes I had watched.

"Listen, they have miracle cures all the time. I thought they should send him away to a sanatorium. Then when the letters came in from my fans, he could have been cured. This way," and I saw the corners of his mouth turn down and knew that he was really unhappy about losing Matt, "they can't ever bring him back."

"I'm sorry," I said. And I was. With Matt gone and *Volpone* closing, he would be free,

which is the actor's way of saying unemployed
— unless he had something else coming up,
which I doubted, since he would surely have told
me about that first.

"It's probably a good thing," he said. "I'll be
able to give all my attention to this." He nodded
at the script. "You're going to love it, hon." He
reached across the table and took my hands.
"We'll be fantastic together. The best father-
and-daughter acting team since . . ."

"Ryan and Tatum O'Neal?" I suggested.

"Exactly."

He did look a little bit like Ryan O'Neal when
he smiled. My mind shot off to long days together on the set, of scenes where we acted,
brilliantly, our own lives. Would there be flashbacks? He could play his younger self, with
make-up, but they would have to find a little
blond girl to be the young me. There weren't
going to be any flashbacks, I decided. I wasn't
going to share him with anyone in our story.

We had to hurry out, since I was due back in
twenty minutes. He dropped me at the studio
gate.

"Thank you for lunch," I said, leaning in the
car window. I couldn't wait to get inside with my
folder. The first break I had, I was going to start
reading.

"Be nice to Boone," my father said. "A lot
depends on his liking this."

"Of course," I said. I was always nice to

Boone. At least lately I had been nice to Boone. "We're going on location. To Lancaster."

"The Foster Ranch?" my father asked.

I tended to forget that he knew about things like that. "Yes. Next week."

"Well," he said, racing the engine a little, "let me know as soon as you can what he thinks of the script."

"I will," I promised, and watched him drive away.

I had lots of breaks that afternoon. I put my father's manuscript inside my script and pretended to be studying my lines.

In the first act the father, a successful movie actor, learns, very unexpectedly, that he has a daughter — by overhearing a conversation in a fancy restaurant. The first act told how he tracked her down through the *Player's Directory* and then through her agent, since he knows she acts in commercials. The mother and a friend (Phyllis?) never appear in the first act; only their voices are heard from the booth behind the actor-father. And of course I wasn't even in the story yet.

In the second act the father discovers that the mother is a terrible person who has kept the existence of the child secret for her own peculiar reasons. He also discovers that he is in danger. That part wasn't very clear to me and I promised myself I would figure it out later. I still hadn't appeared.

154

In the third act I appeared. He has traced me to the set where I am making a commercial for cat food. I am in a corner crying because my mother and the director of the commercial have both been insensitive and cruel to me. He comes to my side and comforts me. "Don't cry, little girl," he begins. "You'll never have to cry again." I look up at him, bewildered. "Fathers," he continues, "never let their little girls cry. And I am your father."

"Oh, yes," the girl says. "Oh, yes." And a few lines later: "But where have you been all this time?"

Unbidden, the image of Peregrine, Gentleman Traveller, flashed into my mind. Feeding straight lines to keep the narrative moving.

In the last act the father confronts the mother and tells her the girl is going to live with him from now on. I am — the little girl in the script is — delirious with joy. It ends with them walking away together, arm in arm.

I closed the folder. Arm in arm. The image stayed with me.

It was rough, but I had expected that. But it wasn't very much like the conversation we had had in my dressing room. It wasn't very much like what had happened. And I hadn't expected that. But he had written it in a great hurry, after all. It was just a first draft. We'd be making changes.

My part was a lot smaller than I had expected.

To be honest, I had imagined myself the star. I could almost hear Boone's voice: "You don't have to be at the center of every scene, Miss Kelley." And my mother's: "Sometimes the small parts are the best."

That was it. I had trouble reading the script because I wasn't the big star in it. And if I had been, what would it have been? A kiddie movie? No, this was right. And it *was* good. Maybe I should show it to my mother before I took it to Boone.

I couldn't do that. She would pick up her pen and start working on the rough places right away. He certainly ought to be allowed to fix the rough places himself. I was sure he knew where they were.

No, I would show it to Boone. On location. That would be the best place to do it. I fiddled with the Beast's control panel, which I had moved into the fantasy center of my mind, and zipped past Boone's reading through his wild enthusiasm for the project to the set on which we would be working, my father and I.

I could do a lot with that scene where the girl is crying. I cry especially well when the script requires it.

The clearest thing that I can say about going on location is that it is an intimate experience. The only people at the Come-Right-Inn, at which we stayed, were us. The whole crew, of course, but no one else. There was a hotel manager and a desk clerk, waitresses in the coffee shop and, no doubt, a cook. An occasional delivery truck would come right up to the Come-Right-Inn, but it would then go right back out. Essentially, we Beauty-and-Beasters made up the entire planet. Maggie Arnold was there, of course, but no planet is ever going to be entirely perfect.

The first day was exciting. We went out onto the desert, about an hour out of the Come-Right-Inn. We traveled in a huge van that held us and a built-in, well-equipped commissary. Behind us were two more huge aluminum-glistening vans, which carried the equipment. When we got to the planet site, the trucks were all parked away from the area that would be used in the shooting. Then the rocky earth and barren cliff before us were turned into our Beast's planet.

CLAPBOARD: ONCE UPON A GALAXY, SCENE 36

[In her bedroom on earth, Beauty dreams. She tosses and moans.

The Beast stands at the opening of a cave, looking out toward the castle. He is stooped and smaller. He hangs his head sorrowfully, turns and walks into the cave, collapses on the ground, moaning and shaking his great head. His breathing is labored and loud.]

[Beauty starts from her sleep, sits upright in her bed.]

Beauty: Beast! Dear Beast! *[Goes to window and looks out.]* I am no longer at home on Earth. I must go home to the Beast.

The Beast, in this dream sequence, lay in a real cave in the desert. It was hot and still inside and Keith had to lie there in his Beast suit and suffer, which he said got easier by the minute. Even though, in the script, the action shifts from Beauty, to the cave, back to Beauty, we really did all of Beauty sleeping at one time, and now all I had to do was rush out onto the desert at night. It was so dark in the cave that there was no need for the special day-to-night lens to shoot Keith's scenes.

At night at the Come-Right-Inn, you either hung out in the coffee shop or in the bar, or you hung out in your room. Or maybe in somebody else's room. But those were the big choices. I knew that I needed to get my father's script to Boone, but the first night there I did not even see him after dinner. I asked Keith if he had any idea where Boone was, and he said he thought probably in his room going over the scenes for the next day.

"He must know the lines," I said.

"Of course he does, Kristin. But there's so much more a director has to do than that."

I wondered.

We were scheduled to be here only five days. On the second day I realized I had to get the script to Boone pretty quickly or he would have

158

no time to read it before we left. That night I looked all over for him and again could not find him anywhere. I doubted that he would be at the bar, because I had heard that he didn't drink, so I concluded that he must again be in his room. And I knew that one did not go and bother the director in his own room. At least I knew that I shouldn't do it.

But then, if I didn't, what would I tell my father had happened to my super plan to have Boone read the script while we were in the desert? We were at dinner when I concluded that action was called for.

Keith seemed to know what I had in mind when I rose from the booth we were sitting in.

"You still looking for Boone?"

"Yes," I said.

"You're not supposed to bother the director when he's not on the set," he said.

Sometimes Keith annoyed me.

"Eat your dessert," I said.

He waved me aside as though we'd never kissed at all. I could never understand how someone you had kissed and in whose arms you had rested could become almost a stranger so quickly. In a sense I never understood how marriages begun truly in love could break up the way they kept doing. With all of the sex that came with the territory of marriage, you would think that too much had been exchanged between two people for them to just have it melt away. That people might have sex and then not marry was obvious, and I had heard enough to know that the whole thing could be achieved in a great spirit of fun and without any thought of love and commitment. That might be, and perhaps that was how I was conceived and why my mother did not want to marry after a fling on the basis of fun-for-now. So many people made love so much of the time to so many people that it was clearly impossible for them all to be seriously in love. Or even thinking of love at all. But when there was love involved, intended to last, enhanced by the incredible knowledge and power that must be transmitted by actually making love — I couldn't see it falling apart.

Even my one kiss with Keith had made him someone I could not have negligible feelings toward. Not so with him, though, I guessed. Keith, of course, had no doubt kissed a million girls, and outside of games at parties and my kisses in my Emmy movie (in which I played a sixteen-year-old and got to think about love and mislove at great length and kissed two different men, with the director telling me what to do with my hands, cheeks and even toes so that it never felt like more than a pose for a camera), I had never seriously kissed anybody as I had seriously kissed Keith.

So, I reflected as I walked up the stairs to Boone's room, Keith was not pure-hearted like the Beast. If I was ever to love the Beast, I would know for sure that he would never go away from me. Not because he was a beast and could find no one else, but because he would know that I loved him truly. And I would know that he loved me truly, for why else would we have worked so hard to finally know each other? I thought about the Beast a lot, for I loved him already and could not understand it taking Beauty all this time to love him.

I walked down the hallway to Boone's door, took a deep breath and knocked. There was no answer, but then, it had been a timid knock. I knocked loudly. Still no answer.

Script under my arm, I stepped back. Was he inside and not answering? If so, I figured I'd best get away quickly and hope he never connected me with the knock. It was only eight o'clock. He couldn't be sleeping.

Where could Boone be?

I went downstairs and double-checked the possibilities inside the hotel. He was not there. That he could be in someone else's room finally occurred to me. And about that I could do nothing. Maybe he'd found three others for a bridge game.

I went out into the desert night. It was cool and clear, stars cluttering the sky. The daytime sage-and-mesquite smells had faded with the heat.

Though I had heard him say once that he did not swim, I thought that perhaps he might be sitting at the pool. Many of the crew had gone swimming when we'd come back from location, but now the pool area was as silent as the night. I walked toward it.

Boone was there. I was walking softly and he did not seem to hear my approach. His back was to me and I saw his head, tilted unusually backward, not in any pose I had come to think of as characteristic of his body. And though he sat on a normal beach chair, designed almost exactly like a director's chair, I could not see his calves or feet as I approached. They just didn't go down that far.

If he was out here, it was surely okay to go up to him.

I continued forward. Just as I was about to speak, I heard a groan and saw his head go forward. I raced up to him. "Boone," I called, seeing his hands twist in pain, gripping each other.

Somehow the sound of my voice was like "Cut!" on the set. He looked up at me calmly, but there was sweat on his forehead and the lines in his usually relaxed face were deep, almost gouged.

"Kristin, good evening. Are you going for a swim this late?"

I wasn't dressed for swimming. That was the only thing that ruined his quick response. When he saw that I realized the strangeness of his question, he immediately went on: "No, of course not. Are you looking for me?"

"Yes."

"You found me."

"Boone, are you in pain?"

"What did you want to ask me, Kristin, that brought you out into this heat?"

He knew me well enough, this man, to know when I was acting and when I was not, even if sometimes I didn't know myself. We both knew this time that I meant what came from my mouth: "Boone, I don't want you to be in pain."

He didn't slough it off again. Or continue the denial. He looked at me and smiled an almost bashful smile. As if he'd been caught in a way he didn't like anyone to see, but that my having found him this way did somehow involve us with each other in a way in which we had not been involved before.

"Sit down, Kristin, why don't you?"

I did.

"Sometimes my hands hurt a lot. Sometimes my arms, sometimes my back."

"What from?"

He laughed. "Let's just say they do their own thing."

"And you'd rather not have anything to do with it," I said.

He laughed again. "Right, Kristin, exactly. And we don't have to have anything to do with them anymore right now. Your coming seems to have sent them off on their own."

I looked at his strong, tiny hands. They were at rest. His brow still dripped with perspiration. I

163

wished I had a handkerchief. I wanted so much to wipe the sweat off his brow. He brushed his forehead with his shirt-sleeve and that took care of that.

I remembered what I had read at UCLA: Sometimes the dwarf has some complication that could lead to paralysis, but surgery was often successful at preventing this.

"Can you do anything about this, Boone? Is there some operation or something?"

He looked at me suspiciously, then acceptingly. "Been doing some reading, Kristin? Yes, I may have to have an operation. Time to change topics, your director says."

I didn't want to change topics. "Do you take pills?" I asked. "When the pain comes?"

"Is this an interview for *Aspirin News*?"

"No, Boone. I just mean it."

He saw I did.

"I do have pills, yes. This time I didn't have them with me. But also this time the pain was less. I'm okay, so let's talk about something else. My pain didn't bring you out here."

"No, I know," I said. "I want to ask you to do me a favor." But I couldn't get the sound of his groan or the sight of his pain out of my thoughts and feelings. "Boone, I would take your pain if I could. I mean — oh, I don't know what I mean."

"You certainly are saying the right things for someone who wants to ask a favor. It could even be a big one."

164

I froze. I couldn't open my mouth. Did he really think that?

He saw what had happened and he saw immediately what he had said. For the first time I heard Boone's voice falter. He reached out toward me, and the hand that had writhed before touched my elbow in a gentle and caressing way.

"God, sometimes I'm an idiot. I'm so sorry, Kristin. I didn't mean that the way it sounded. Or worse, I did mean it the way it sounded, but I know you didn't mean that at all. That's what pain can do, I know. Block out what's real and what isn't. You're real and you meant to help. Forgive me."

I reached out my hand and touched one of the deep creases in his cheek. I knew he wouldn't want me to cry, but I was close. We just stayed that way for at least a minute. Then he spoke and his voice was together again and he said, "Thank you, Kristin. Now tell me about the favor you want. Your chances are good, I'd say."

"Star billing," I said. "Above the Beast's. No, above the director's."

He laughed. "Never, never, not that."

He was seeing me more clearly now. His eyes were clear, the humor was back, the show would go on.

"What doth Beauty carry under her arm?"

"The favor," I said.

"Oh, God, you've written a script. You want me to read a script you've written? You're fourteen years old and you want me to produce and direct your first Broadway show?"

"I didn't write it," I said. "And you only have to read it and tell me what you think of it. You don't have to sign any run-of-the-play contracts before reading."

"Who wrote it?" he asked warily. "Oh, no, of course, your mother. It's a romance set on the Beast's planet. She wants you to do your first adult role."

"Don't pick on my mother," I said, "or she'll put you in a book."

"Hah, hah, more likely a short story." He moaned, as if the line had been too good to resist.

"No, not my mother, and I'm not going to tell you right now who wrote it. You said you'd do me a favor. I just want a reading and an opinion."

"I never get into this situation, Kristin. Not for years. Tell me at least that no one I know wrote it, or I will not read it. I cannot be objective about the writing of people I know. That is an unfortunate failing, but it is one of the many I have."

"No one you know wrote it."

"Okay. Give it to me."

I handed it to him, glad that I had taken out the title page. "I thought you'd have time while we're on location . . . that it would be a good time for you."

"In other words, could I read it tonight and get

166

right back to you?'' He was his old self; we'd stepped back from that precipice of intimacy. I answered with my old self, ''That would be nice, if you could work it into your schedule.''

''We'll see. Now you go back and work sleep into your schedule, or Beauty will have marks under the camera's eyes tomorrow.''

''You're staying here?''

''Any business of yours?'' he asked.

''None,'' I said, and walked off.

How it was that Adam Michael Boone had become business of mine I don't know, but I walked off that desert as slowly as I could, listening intently, praying not to hear the sound of pain coming with me across the night air.

We caught up the next day with all the outdoor shots that would be combined during editing with those we'd already done on the sound stage. Beauty had only one more scene.

At dinner I hovered over Boone. He said nothing to me that indicated we'd ever discussed a script at all. He got up to go, not staying for dessert, and walking by me, said very softly, ''See you at the pool in an hour.''

I was there in much less than an hour. Nights on the desert must be always one and the same, for again tonight the smell of the day's heat lingered and the light hung on and on, making the darkness that finally settled almost an afterthought.

He finally came out. As I watched him move toward me, I wondered if he was still in pain. If it was so, I could not tell. He seemed as he had on the set that afternoon, completely involved with the present, uninvolved with his body.

He lifted himself into the same chair he had sat in the previous night. I tried to convince him that I was not, for the thousandth time, noticing the way he was. But no matter how long I knew Boone, I realized, I would always see the distortion. The best that I could do was to try, over and over again, to have this expression of not noticing anything out of the ordinary on my face.

Boone settled back in the chair and smiled at me. "You going to stand up?"

I walked over to the pool and got another chair and came back and sat down opposite him.

"I read it," he said, and hesitated.

I sat forward. "Yes?"

"You didn't write it, right?"

"No. I told you that."

"I feel a need to run through it again, I guess." I waited.

"Your mother didn't write it?"

"Come on, Boone. What'd you think of it?"

"It's terrible."

I was totally unprepared. He could tell me that my acting in some scene was terrible, he could correct anything about me. And he was always right. I had finally learned that. But that the script was terrible?

"No," I said.

"Unfortunately, yes," he said. "Look, Kristin, this is why I never read scripts. I hate to tell anyone that something is terribly written."

"You're wrong," I said.

He looked at me and sighed. "Well, I could be wrong. Anyone can be wrong."

"You could be wrong," I said, but we both heard the question mark in my voice.

"Not really, Kristin. Somebody could like it, I guess. Someone's mother, brothers, cousins, friends, lovers, strangers — anyone could like it. But it's terrible."

I was already holding back tears. I am always so prepared for anything — but on the subject of my father I seemed to have gone haywire.

"Why is it terrible?" I asked.

He had the script in his hand.

"Oh, Kristin, for goodness' sake, listen." He opened the script and read:

Father: All of my life, all of these years that I didn't know that you existed, I thought about you, missed you, wondered what you would be like if you did exist. In my head I would take you to Disneyland, Catalina, the museums, the zoo, the amusement parks. Every day I thought about the daughter I didn't know I had.

Boone read it straight, just the way it was on the page. Then he flipped a few pages, looked for something else, found it.

Father: I will make up to you for all the years we have missed. You have brought meaning back into my life.

The last one clinched it. Boone said, "And listen to this mother character":

Mother: All these years, Stanton, I have deprived our daughter of two parents. I can only apologize to you both. I should have known better, should have done better.

He stopped and looked at me with an expression of dismay on his face. "How could you like this? People don't talk like that, think like that. This is unreal. Phony. That's what I mean by 'terrible.' To be honest, I would have thought you'd recognize it."

Hearing him read the lines, I had indeed recognized it. But who had I been when I read the script alone, when my father had brought it to me?

"Do I need to read more?" he asked.

"No," I answered.

He handed me the script. He was finished. So was I. An actress always knows how she looks. I looked crestfallen. And defenseless. And I couldn't look any other way.

"What I can't understand," Boone said gently, more gently than I'd ever heard him speak or suspected that this director could speak, "is why you think this is good."

He deserved an answer. I couldn't think of anything but the truth. "Boone, remember what you said about mothers and aunts and uncles and everyone liking a writer's work?"

"Yes."

"My father wrote it."

"Ah," he said, and the pain on his face, which could only have been there because of what we were saying to each other, was the same pain I had seen the night before, when it was physical agony in his body. I started to cry.

"Poor Kristin," he said, and he rested his hand on my hair. "I'm so sorry."

I cried and he didn't give me any directions to stop or go on or which way to face the camera. He just kept his hand on my head. In the midst of my tears it occurred to me to ask him a question.

"Boone?" I asked through the sniffling.

"Yes, Kristin."

"Did you ever act in *Volpone*?"

"Yes, I did."

I cried harder. I guess he thought it was time to step in and be the director again.

"I played Volpone," he said and started to laugh. I looked up at him. I stopped crying. I started to laugh.

"Come closer, Kristin," he said. I stood up, leaned down over him. He kissed me on the tip of my nose. "Let's call it a take, shall we?" he said.

I nodded, somehow back in balance again.

We walked back silently.

Now what was I going to tell my father?

Getting ready for bed, I kept wondering how to tell my father that Boone did not like his script. He would be so hurt and his hopes for us would be so dashed. Well, I had a few days to think of what to say and how to say it. Meanwhile, I also had Keith, the Beast and Beauty very much on my mind. When I got into bed I fell asleep.

The next day, despite the heat and the strangeness of the desert, things went so smoothly that we had time to run through the following day's scene, the final one, the transformation.

"Call it a wrap," Boone said. "Nice work, everybody."

We drove back to the motel in a very companionable silence. Everything was going well. We would finish shooting the next day. The picture felt good, and that is a nice feeling for people on location. It's somehow different from just being on the set in the city. After all, we'd been on a different planet together.

Boone and I were walking slowly together toward the entrance of the motel when I saw my father. What on earth was I supposed to do now? Why on earth had he come to the location? How would I explain him? If I could have decided what performance to give, it would have been easy, but I couldn't.

"What's wrong? Kristin?" Boone asked.

I looked at him. Speechless. "I . . ."

"Look, Kristin. I think we know each other better than I usually know people. What is it? You look awful."

Again I tried: "I . . ."

Entrance: Howard Glendon.

He strode right up to us. The rest of the crew had gone in, and there were just the three of us, under the hot sun outside the motel.

"Hi, sweetheart," he said, bending and kissing me on the cheek. He looked so cool, so handsome, hardly in need of air conditioning.

Then, "Hello there, Adam Michael Boone. Long time no see."

Boone shook hands with my father, clicking it all in. I could almost see the pieces falling into place in his brilliant mind. "Ages," he said. "How are things, Glendon?"

"Great. Very good. Lots coming up. New series, it looks like."

"Good. You've waited awhile."

"We were both in *Volpone*," my father told me. "A few years back."

"I played a dwarf," Boone said and winked at me. "What are you doing up here?"

My father hesitated. I think he decided to be cautious. "I came to see Kristin," he said.

Boone asked no further questions, but he continued to talk.

"Kristin's great to know," he said. "Look, why don't you join us for dinner?"

"I'd love to," my father said.

"I'm starved," Boone said. "Let's just go in, get a booth and eat, okay?"

"Fine," I said.

"Wonderful," my father said.

Usually everyone washed and changed before dinner, so this early the coffee shop was almost empty and we were immediately sitting in a round booth, chatting. Boone chatting was something else again. He was just not a man who wasted words, but he went on about the old days when he started out, and did my father remember so-and-so, and on and on.

Then, every once in a while, he would be quiet and wait for my father to say something. Finally my father gave Boone the cue he'd been waiting for. He asked, "Are you glad you went into directing?"

Boone smiled. "I am so glad. You know, I used to write. I'm so glad I gave it up. It's got to be the hardest art of them all, although I know Kristin's mother here does it about twenty-four hours a day. Still, I would have written plays and that's about the hardest thing to do. Just a few days ago I read a new play; in fact, Kristin showed it to me, by one of her friends, and it was a well-meaning but unproducible sort of work. I didn't like it at all and imagine Kristin's friend — I suspect a romance," he said, and again winked at me, "won't be too happy when she tells him how dreadful I thought it was. Maybe the writer's very young and will get better. Or maybe the
174

writer will go into some other field. Anyway, reading it made me decide I was glad I hadn't continued writing."

The waitress came up. "Dessert?" she asked.

"Not for me," Boone said. "I've got to go. Why don't you and Howard have dessert, Kristin? Are you staying overnight, Howard?"

"I don't know," my father said.

"It was good seeing you," Boone said and shook hands with my father and walked slowly off, having given, as far as I am concerned, the finest performance of his career. I still didn't know just what to say, but I sure didn't have to worry about how I would say it. Thank you, Boone.

We ordered shakes.

"I'm sorry, Dad, really sorry."

"At least you didn't tell him I wrote it," my father said. "What does he know? He knows nothing."

"Well, Dad, I don't think you can say that."

"He only got where he is because he's a dwarf and people feel sorry for him."

No wonder my mother hadn't wanted to marry this man.

I said nothing.

"We'll get it produced, don't worry," he said.

"I don't want to do it," I said.

"What?"

"It's not a good part for me."

He looked at me, his blue eyes wide and

175

startled and pained. He looked like a child who had just been told he wasn't going to Disneyland after all. And who couldn't believe that life was so unfair. So much, I thought, for the patient, loving father who was going to take me to Disneyland and Magic Mountain. I was much too old for that anyway.

"Did you talk to your mother about this? Was it her idea?"

"No," I said. "I make my own decisions about my career."

He had a mobile actor's face, transparent, the emotions shining right through. I did too, I knew, but I thought I could control it. Sometimes the emotions you were feeling weren't the ones you needed to have showing. Like those on his face at that moment: anger and disappointment and then a sort of peevish fury. The thought in his head was so plain he might as well have said it: What about *my* career?

"I don't think I can help you," I said. "Not with this."

The faintest glimmer of hope flickered across his face and I realized what I had said. If not with this, maybe with something else.

"Maybe I'll rewrite this. Make your part bigger."

I almost laughed at how close he had come to my first thought about his script. We were both actors for sure.

"I don't think that would help, Dad. A bigger
176

part in a bad play isn't really any better than a small part. Maybe worse." I didn't want him to rewrite the script, maybe coming back again and again with different terrible versions. I didn't think about it sounding cruel until I saw that he had reddened slightly. He picked up the script and stood up.

"Maybe there will be something else we can be in together," I heard myself saying. I couldn't bear the look on his face. I hadn't meant to be so blunt.

His face lightened immediately. "That would be nice," he said. "You work on that. And I'll see what I can arrange."

"Good-by, Dad." I was afraid that he was going to sit down again and start reviewing possible vehicles for the two of us. "I have to get to bed early. We start shooting in the morning."

"Of course." He rolled the script up in his hands. "I understand." He turned to leave. "I'll be in touch," he said, and walked out of the restaurant.

I went to bed and studied my lines for the next day. Whatever Howard Glendon might be doing, I was finishing *Once upon a Galaxy* in the morning and I needed to be prepared and to get plenty of sleep. Without dreams. As far as I could tell, those had pretty much ended. I had traded a perfect dream father, one who could be — and had been — anything I wanted, for a real father, one who could only be what he was.

[5] Last Scene: The Prince

CLAPBOARD: ONCE UPON A GALAXY, SCENE 38

[Beauty twists the ring and is instantly back in the main room of the castle, looking out of the window. She rushes frantically about, looking for the Beast, and then goes into the desert, remembering the dream.]

The rushing frantically about we had done at the studio on the castle set, and now, on location, I was outside looking for the Beast's cave. It was hot and my dress clung to me. We had to stop every few minutes for wardrobe to fiddle with the dress and make-up with my face and the hairdresser with my hair. At least I wasn't Keith in that terrible Beast suit in this heat.

I had discovered a lot of new things about myself. I didn't like heat, at least not heat like this, and I was terrified of scorpions. Maggie Arnold had found one in her room at the motel and come screaming for help. I was convinced as I stumbled over the hot sand that there was a scorpion

— probably entire families of scorpions — behind every rock or rise in the earth.

I was embarrassed about my fear. I had to confess it to Boone when he called "Cut!" for the tenth time because he didn't like the way I was running.

"You are frantic to find the dying Beast," Boone said.

"Yes," I agreed.

"Then, Kristin, why are you *tiptoeing*?"

"Scorpions."

Boone laughed and laughed. "I would never have suspected," he said at last, "that *you* would be afraid of such a little thing as that."

"It's not the only little thing I'm afraid of," I said, "or I wouldn't be running at all."

Boone waved his hand at all the people standing around. "In all the time we've been here, has any one of these people ever been stung by a scorpion?"

"I thought they bit."

"They sting. Has any one of them seen a scorpion on the desert?"

"Maggie Arnold did. In her room."

"Ah." Boone nodded. "In her *room*, Kristin. May I ask you? Do you go to your room and tiptoe there all night?"

"No," I said. "But I will from now on."

Just then Keith came out in his Beast suit. He'd been waiting in one of the air-conditioned

179

trailers — the only place the suit was bearable —
to be called. Boone explained that it might be a
little while because Beauty was tiptoeing to the
Beast's rescue because she was afraid of scorpions.

"Hey, Kristin," Keith said, "I'm glad you
mentioned that." He turned to Boone. "I was
worried about tarantulas. Do you realize I could
be *covered* by tarantulas and nobody would
notice for hours?"

Boone and I looked at the Beast suit and then
at each other. It was true. The suit, in fact,
looked a lot like a collection of tarantulas.

Keith plucked at the suit and jumped around.
"I got one," he shouted. "And another."

"Don't get near me," I screamed, backing
away.

"Here, catch," Keith yelled and made a
throwing gesture toward me.

"Got it," I yelled and turned to Boone and
threw underhanded.

Boone held his ground bravely. He caught at
empty air, his little hands crossing each other in
space. There was only the smallest of hesitations
before he whirled to Keith, tossed and shouted,
"Put that tarantula *back*! He was covering a bald
spot."

I didn't exactly lose my fear of scorpions, but I
stopped tiptoeing enough to satisfy Boone. He
decided that my residual fear gave just the right
degree of urgency to my running.

CLAPBOARD: ONCE UPON A GALAXY,
SCENE 39

[Cave in the desert: Beauty hesitates at the entrance, then goes inside, where she finds the Beast, weak, dying. She rushes to him, kneels at his side.]

Beauty: Beast. Speak to me. Please. Please say something.

Beast: *[Opens eyes painfully.]* Beauty? Is it you?

Beauty: I'm sorry I was gone so long.

Beast: You came back to me. *[Sighs and closes his eyes.]*

Beauty: *[Cries.]* My Beast is dead. And it is all my fault. Poor Beast. *[She tries to lift his head, cradles it in her arms.]* I love you, Beast. Don't leave me. *[She bends and kisses the Beast tenderly, sadly.]*

Then, when Boone said "Cut," I could not move. I had to stay in the same position until it was marked exactly, so that when Keith changed from the Beast suit to his Prince rags — which is what he called the elegant black-and-silver suit he wore in this scene — we could take the precise positions with which the scene had ended.

I was glad that I had to stay still. Beauty's sorrow for the Beast had somehow slipped out of her and into me. I felt real grief at the thought of the dying Beast. I understood what Boone had been trying to tell me earlier, when I was babbling about Beauty as a feminist symbol.

"It's sort of late to finally understand," I told

Boone as he came to stand by my side and pat my arm.

"I think you understood all the time, Kristin," he said. "At least some part of you understood. Because Beauty always knew."

"I have a better ending."

"You do, do you? Tell us how you'll improve over the already improved-upon *Blue Fairy Book*."

"When she kisses him," I said, "he can stay exactly as he is. His turning into the handsome Prince is silly. It's meaningless."

"Meaningless, my foot," Keith said, walking up just at that moment. "I'd miss my best scene."

Boone looked at Keith, tall and handsome in the Prince suit, then at me. I had never seen him look so content as he did just then. As though someone had brought him flowers. Dozens of perfect red roses. I thought surely he would overrule Keith and do it my way, but when he spoke it was to reject my idea.

"That's an interesting idea, Kristin," he said very formally, so formally that I wondered what it was that he wasn't saying. "But I think we'd better stick to realism. The Beast is kissed, the charm is broken and we have a handsome Prince."

"Hurrah for me," Keith said.

"It's the way the script goes," Boone said.

"Let's break for lunch and try to finish up this afternoon."

[Cave in the desert: Beauty cries as she holds the Beast's head in her lap. The Beast slowly changes, his face and head blurring and shrinking, and then the Prince is there, looking up at Beauty.]

Keith, now in the silver and black of the Prince, took his place, settling exactly into the marks that indicated where the Beast had been. I arranged myself carefully in the spot where I had kneeled above the Beast. And we began the last scene of the movie.

Prince: A spell. A spell older than time.

Beauty: Magic.

Prince: All that I tried to end my enchantment, and you have ended it with a simple kiss.

[They rise and embrace. They kiss. They leave the cave and walk over the desert toward the castle.]

We were finished. The movie was over. I was excited, but there was also an emptiness inside. I hugged Keith. Boone came over and I hugged him, too.

"The change," I said. "That was the special effect I didn't see?"

Boone just smiled.

LAST DETAIL ON THE MYSTERY OF MY EXISTENCE

My mother was actually waiting for me when the big vans pulled into the Twentieth Century parking lot. I said good-bye to everyone and ran up to her.

"Hop in," she said. "We're having dinner out."

"Great," I said. "Some solid restaurant food after days of desert rations."

"You know, Kristin, I'm a little surprised to find that I feel this so strongly, but this location business . . . I think I'd prefer you to postpone any long trips — Paris or whatever — till you're older. Or till I'm older. I missed you."

I was speechless. But joyful.

"Any news of your recently discovered father?" she asked.

I hesitated. The desert and my disappointment came back.

"He completed the script, Mother."

"Really?" She was thoughtful. "Well, I was wrong."

"It's awful," I said.

"Well, I was right."

"He's pretty unhappy with me."

"Why?"

"I told him I didn't like it. That I didn't want to be in it."

"Howard never wanted to hear the truth about anything, especially about himself."

184

Suddenly I wanted to protect this Howard I had tracked for so long.

"He'll do another," I said. "He said he'd keep in touch."

"Maybe," she said.

"Well, he might."

"I'm not saying no." I could see she was sad.

"He's not too, too . . ." I hesitated.

"Strong?" she said.

I nodded. I thought I was going to cry.

"You're not the only one, you know," she said.

"Who what?"

"Who fell for him. Remember this, although I've managed never to think of it except to pride myself on my wise decision at such a young age: I was madly in love with Howard Glendon. Never wonder, Kristin, about one thing: You were conceived in love and I never doubted that I wanted you. It's embarrassing to look back at loving Howard, but you are, after all, a great addition to the world."

"I am?"

Blues to blues. "You've always seemed to know that."

"Bravado, Mother. Pure bravado."

"Really?"

"Really."

She nodded. I could sense we couldn't go on too long with the discussion because one of her characters was bound to be lying around loose somewhere, waiting for Mother's return to get his day going. I started to draw back.

"Are you glad you found him, Kristin?"

I hadn't expected that question. I thought a minute. "I don't know. I guess I liked the stunt man better."

"So did I," she said.

I thought that was the end of the conversation, but then she went on: "If he does keep in touch, Kristin . . . you'll have to handle that."

What if he keeps asking me for things? went through my head. The thought frightened me.

"Will you help me, Mother?" I couldn't remember asking my mother for anything before.

She looked surprised, but pleased.

"If I can," she said. "But I don't think I'll have to. You get your strength from our side of the family."

We'd been back from location a few days when Boone called to change the time we had arranged to reshoot those scenes — parts of scenes, actually — in which he needed new angles.

"I think," he said over the phone, "if you can make it on such short notice, I'd like to do them tomorrow. I've lined up everyone else."

"I thought you were going to play in some bridge tournament."

"That didn't work out. Can you make it tomorrow?"

"Of course." I hadn't anything special planned. Besides, I wanted to ask Boone something and I'd just as soon get it over with.

We met, the next day, on the same sound stage we had used before, the sets looking faded to me now after the reality of the desert. He directed me in standing, sitting, turning, while the lights flicked on and off and the cameras rolled.

From the first day of shooting, Boone had sat in a special chair, higher than the average chair, so that he could see the set and all the actors. The first week I had been fascinated by his willingness to climb down it laboriously, come to the set to talk to us, return to his chair and scramble up again every time he felt he needed to.

Today, however, he climbed into the chair in the morning and stayed there until we broke for lunch. He shouted at us or sent Mike, the assistant director, to relay instructions.

When we broke for lunch, everyone seemed to drift tactfully away as Boone climbed down from the chair. Everyone but me. I stood and watched as he turned and backed slowly down the height. He dropped the last few inches, hit the floor with a thud and at once tightened his hands on the chair seat. I could see his fingers pale with the strength of his grasp.

He turned and saw me. "Kristin!" He sounded annoyed and embarrassed.

"What's the matter, Boone?"

"Nothing."

"Boone," I said, "it's me, Kristin, from the desert."

He paused, then nodded. "I do seem to have something wrong with my back," he admitted. "But it's only temporary."

I was enormously relieved. "I want to ask you something. Could we talk for a minute?" It would have been easier just to ask, but I was suddenly very shy.

"Let's sit down, then," Boone said. He sat on the edge of a bench at the back of the studio, his legs sticking out in front of him. I sat next to him.

"Yes?"

"It's about the Emmys."

"No."

I started. "No, what do you mean 'no'? I haven't asked you anything yet."

"No, I don't know if you've won. And if I did I wouldn't tell you."

"That's not what I wanted to ask. They're soon, you know. And my mother, you know my mother."

"I know your mother and I know the Emmys are soon. What I don't know is the connection."

"She really doesn't want to go. And I have to go with someone."

Boone looked at me. "Read that line again. I'm not sure if it's 'I have to go *with* someone,' 'I have to *go* with someone,' or 'I have to go with *someone*.'"

My face was red. I could not look at him. This

was turning out to be much more difficult than I had imagined, and I was doing a very bad job besides. "I wondered, if you were going, maybe we could go together. Unless you already have plans to take someone else." That was approximately what I had originally planned to say. I hadn't known it would sound so bald.

"Well," he said. "Well. I'm very flattered. And no, I have no plans to take anyone to the ceremony."

I looked up. He was looking away from me, back toward the darkened set.

"Because," he went on, "I am not going to go I have other plans. Plans I can't change. That operation you asked me about, remember? i have to have it."

"When?" I demanded.

"Friday morning."

"May I visit you?" I really wanted to know if I could be right in the operating room with him so that I could watch every minute and be sure he was okay.

"I won't be good company," he warned. "I do a marvelous hospital patient, except that he's a very irritable, grouchy character."

"I'll take my chances," I said. "Will this fix everything?"

"Not everything," Boone said, laughing. "I'll still be a dwarf. But the doctors seem to think it will fix my back."

Then I felt his hand touch mine, rest on mine.

189

"But, Kristin, if I were going to the awards, I would be so delighted to escort you." He stood up to face me. Even that way, with me still seated, I looked down just a bit into his eyes. He smiled. "Think of the publicity," he said. "*Beauty and the Beast*. Or our next movie, *Snow White and the Dwarf Star!*"

"I'm sorry you can't go," I said. "I really wanted — "

"I know," he said quickly, before I could finish the sentence. "Since the most sophisticated older man you know is unavailable, would you consider a callow youth?"

"Who?"

"Keith. I have just learned" — his voice took on the staccato delivery of a Hollywood gossip columnist with unnerving accuracy — "from a reliable source that Hollywood's newest teenage heart throb *doesn't have a date for the Emmys* because he's been too shy to ask a certain rising young actress and Emmy nominee if she has plans for that evening."

"Really?" Asking Keith, or letting him know I was interested in going with him, had never occurred to me, mostly because I wanted to go with Boone, but partly because it also never occurred to me that Keith didn't have six or seven dates already. "I suppose I could."

Boone laughed. "I was flattered before, but now! Let me suggest that if you do mention this to Keith, you show a bit more enthusiasm. He
190

probably doesn't need to know what a poor second he is to his devastating director."

I began to laugh. With relief, because this was the old Boone and because he was right. From my reaction, he might have been suggesting that I ask some producer's totally unattractive cousin to escort me instead of Keith. "I can manage that," I said.

"Keith's a good person," Boone said, serious again, before he added, "except for his peculiar determination to be a doctor rather than an actor."

"Hard to forgive, isn't it?"

"Almost impossible."

Boone turned away. "I'll see you on the set," he said. As soon as his back was turned to me, he added, "Thank you, Kristin."

"You're welcome," I said to his back, and understood that he wanted me to leave. So I did.

Boone must have gotten to Keith that same evening, because early the next morning Keith called me.

"Hi," I said.

He cleared his throat. "Kristin?"

"Yes?"

"I was wondering. About the Emmys?"

"Yes?"

"If you haven't made any other plans, that is, if you aren't already going with someone . . ."

He knew perfectly well I wasn't going with anyone. Boone must have told him. But it was

191

good for me to hear him having as much trouble as I had had in asking Boone.

"Yes?"

"Would you go with me?" he finished desperately.

"Yes."

"Whew," he said.

I was glad that was settled. "Keith, do you know about Boone's operation?"

"Yes."

"He says it's going to be okay. What do you think?"

"Sure. He's been expecting it for a while. Lots of people have back surgery and they're fine."

We said good-bye. I had a date for the Emmys and Keith's optimism reassured me on Boone's condition.

My mother *really* didn't want to go to the Emmys. When I had told Boone that, it was a statement based more on my knowledge of my mother than on any specific information. As soon as she found out I was going with Keith, her relief was obvious.

"Good," she said. "Then you won't need me there."

"Not unless you'd like to come with us."

"I'll watch at home."

Once my mother decides to do something like shop for clothes for me, she has to get it over with right away. She had Phyllis and me organized early the next day, and we went to Bullock's Wilshire, Magnin's, Saks, Bonwit Teller. I tried on a million dresses while Phyllis and my mother said things about chronological versus psychological versus emotional age as they looked at me. The trick seemed to be finding a dress in which these three ages of mine were as close together as possible. And which also fit and was the right color. I figured we'd still be looking the week after the Emmys.

We finally picked a simple royal-blue silk dress with a high neckline, a pleated bodice and a full skirt. Phyllis made the final choice, since everything my mother picked was too childish and the ones I wanted were, my mother thought, too sophisticated. I could see why Phyllis was a successful agent. She negotiated so well. My mother agreed to the dress, which she thought too old for me, because I promised to wear my hair down, not up as I had wanted, while I agreed to wear my hair down and to the dress because Phyllis persuaded my mother that I should be allowed to wear earrings.

They were both so pleased with themselves about the dress that they let me pick out shoes — very high heels and a tangle of thin, shiny straps that made my feet look elegant rather than just long and skinny — and a bag, also shiny.

Two days later Keith called.

"My mother says I should bring you flowers," he said.

"Oh?" I hadn't thought of that. I wasn't sure flowers would go on the dress. I would have to ask Phyllis. Instead of answering, I asked, "What are you going to wear?"

"I'm going to wear a tuxedo."

"Oh?" I never thought of Keith except in the Beast suit or his Prince rags.

"Are you?" he said.

We both started to laugh. I loved the excitement I could feel building.

Just a week before the Emmys, Boone went into the hospital for his surgery. I called about three times that day. He was fine, they told me, and could have visitors the next day. When I told my mother I was going to visit him, she seemed to think it was a good idea.

"You'll be all right alone, won't you?"

I nodded. Mother hates hospitals. When Phyllis had an operation, my mother called her every day, sometimes twice, and they talked for hours. But she never went to the hospital to see Phyllis.

Boone was at St. John's Hospital, which is maybe two miles from my house. I could take the bus, walk or ride my bike.

I took my bike, concentrating, as I pedaled, on looking older, since I wasn't sure how old you had to be to visit patients.

I found his room on the orthopedic floor with
194

no trouble and stood outside the closed door. A nurse came out. "May I go in?" I asked.

"Of course. Just don't stay too long."

He had a private room. There were flowers all over. I hadn't thought of bringing flowers. Not that they were needed.

"Boone?"

His face lit up and he said hoarsely, "Kristin? How did you find me?"

"It wasn't hard," I said.

"Don't say anything funny. I can't move."

The words hit me right away and their effect must have showed on my face.

"I mean, I'm not supposed to move," he said quickly. "I could except for that."

"Are you going to be all right?"

"Well, you can see they didn't fix everything . . ."

I made a face.

"But they think it will work. With a rigorous therapy program, I can probably compete in the Olympics. Not the long jump, maybe, but — "

"Certainly the high jump."

"No. The hop, skip and jump, I think. That's my event."

I relaxed. He was the old Boone. He was going to be all right. We talked a little longer — he was going to be there about ten days, nothing hurt yet, he was sure the food was going to delay his recovery, the nurses were very nice — until I could see that he was getting tired. I promised to come back every day. "I mean, it's just a ten-minute bike ride and I don't have anything else to do, now that the movie's over. I might as well."

And I did visit. It was good to see him getting stronger every day, to see him first sit up in bed, then put his legs over the side and finally take a few steps, a nurse at his side.

The day before the Emmys I did not visit until late in the afternoon because Keith and I had to attend a long rehearsal of the next night's performance. Seating arrangements were run through, and anything that might come up the next night was anticipated and explained. It was exciting and I was glad I'd have something interesting to tell Boone about when we visited later.

The longer Boone was in the hospital, the more people heard about his operation, and the more people came to visit him. When I went over that afternoon of the Emmy rehearsal, there were three other visitors in with him. Boone had piles of magazines and newspapers surrounding him on the bed.

"My visitors decided I should be kept abreast of the world and supplied me with a year's reading material," he said.

He introduced me to his friends, none of whom were show-business people, but all of whom were obviously friends who cared deeply for Boone.

I am shy with new people and wanted to leave after a few minutes. Boone was in a good mood.

Holding up a magazine and a newspaper, he said, "I've been counting.

"The score, among people who predict such things, is three for you, four for Laura Martin, one for Angela Craig, two assorted ties and two undecided."

He stopped for breath and then went on: "But you're going to win. I know it."

I wish I could have felt as sure.

As we left that day, Boone said, "Don't come tomorrow."

"Why not?"

"Stay home. Rest. Be beautiful. It's a big day for you."

I didn't want to, but I agreed. He'd used his director's voice.

That night, trying to fall asleep, I became convinced that I was not going to win, that Boone's "score" had been right. And I wanted to win. Very much.

I must have fallen asleep finally, because the next morning arrived — the day of the Emmys.

I discovered that it takes a lot of the thrill out of getting dressed in a long silk dress, jewels, high heels and a shiny purse and being met by a handsome man in a tuxedo when you have to go out into the bright sunlight rather than into a dark evening. I felt foolish rather than glamorous.

And Keith — he looked so gorgeous that I knew that not only was I not going to win the Emmy, but that no one would notice that I

197

hadn't. He and my mother kissed each other like old friends. I have never been able to figure out how she meets the people I know and gets to know them, but somehow she does.

We had a car, provided by the studio, that was going to take us to the Shubert in the proper style.

"Your rocket, Beauty," Keith said, bowing me into the back seat.

I giggled. For some reason the long black car, Keith looking like a man instead of a boy, my long dress, the fancy shoes, all made me feel younger rather than older. I was, as I settled into the deep seat, maybe eight years old.

Despite yesterday's rehearsal, we still had to be at the theater long before the program actually began. There were cameras and people from the different television networks there to interview us. And we had to find our seats. The cameras would have to know where we would be sitting so that when the right category came up, they could pick each of us out of the crowd.

"They want to catch the winners smirking and the losers pouting," my mother had said just as we were leaving. "So smile, whatever happens." I promised.

It was still warm, the afternoon sun making my purse shimmer and my hands perspire. Keith held my hand tightly as we arrived, got out and walked toward the entrance and the banks of lights and cameras. There were people waiting on both sides of the theater entrance, fans with autograph books and pictures and albums and pencils. Many of them seemed to be girls about my age, and most of those rushed toward Keith. He signed and smiled and then someone put a book in my hands and I signed and smiled. There were uniformed security guards who gently edged their way between us and the people, letting us move toward the cameras. No one really minded because, right on schedule, someone else pulled up at the curb and drew all the attention.

"Here they come, ladies and gentlemen, two of the brightest young — and I do mean *young* — stars, Kristin Kelley, this year's youngest Emmy nominee, and her handsome escort, Keith Winslow." The interviewer whipped the microphone around with the air of someone producing rabbits from a hat. Keith winked at me and I smiled at the man.

"Well, young lady, are you excited about this evening?"

"Very excited." Surely I could do better than that as an answer. "This is the most exciting thing that's ever happened to me." I felt Keith's hand folding over mine.

"Now, Kristin, what do you think of your chances of winning the Emmy?" He thrust the microphone at me quickly, as if he hoped to surprise an answer from me. I waited modestly.

"Not great," I said exactly at the same moment as Keith said, "She's going to win."

I looked up at him in surprise. "I am?"

"Of course you are," he said.

"Now, that's a testimonial if I ever heard one," the interviewer said. "And who should know better? I understand you just finished a picture with Kristin."

"We did, George," Keith said.

George. That was his name. Trust Keith to remember.

"*Once upon a Galaxy*, George," I said. "Keith's a prince."

"She's Beauty," Keith added, squeezing my hand.

"Actually, he's the Beast," I said, squeezing back. I was now about six years old and regressing rapidly.

George turned slightly away from us and faced the cameras. "I'm sure that from his hospital bed, the very seriously ill Adam Michael Boone will be watching the Emmys tonight if he can and hoping that his young star wins."

I was a hundred years old in an instant. Fire and ice through me.

I heard myself saying through a haze, "I'm sure he is." I turned toward the cameras with a fixed smile. "Hi, Boone."

"Well, I think they're waiting for you inside. Good luck, Kristin. Look forward to the new picture, Keith." George turned away toward the new arrivals and I turned to Keith.

"What did he mean, Keith? Boone was fine

when I saw him yesterday. He called me this morning. To wish me luck.''

Keith pulled me into the lobby, away from the people. "I never thought he'd mention it like that. On camera. You handled it so well.''

I was furious and terrified. "Stop treating me like a baby, Keith." I knew I was acting like one, I was so frightened. "What's the matter with Boone?''

"I called the hospital just before I picked you up," he said slowly. "They wouldn't let me talk to him. My dad called and talked to his doctor. Boone had a pulmonary embolism about noon.''

"What's *that*?" I asked, close to tears.

"A blood clot that goes to the lungs.''

"Is it serious? Is he very sick?''

Keith looked at me and I saw that he was as frightened as I. "Yes, it's serious. Yes, he's very sick, Kristin.''

"Will he die?''

"My dad says . . ." Keith stopped and then went on slowly, picking each word: "Boone didn't die right away, so he's got a good chance. They can treat him.''

I wanted to cry and scream, I was so angry at Boone for not being well, as he'd promised. "Why didn't you tell me, Keith? Why did you let me come here?" I looked around the lobby, which was filling with people in fancy dresses and black suits.

"You're going to win, Kristin. I thought you'd

want to be here. I didn't want anything to spoil it for you."

"I can't stay, Keith." I walked to the door of the central aisle and looked down at the rows of maroon plush seats. Maybe a third of them were filled with people who sat and talked and called across the empty rows to their friends.

The stage was ready for the ceremony. There were three staggered curtains, metallic red and gold and shiny black, and a shallow silver staircase that slanted across the stage and disappeared between two of the curtains.

In the center was a curved dais.

That's where I would stand when I won, cameras on me. People would adore me. Photographers would not be able to take enough pictures of me.

"Kristin?" Keith said behind me.

I didn't move. My eyes were on the dais.

"Stay, Kristin. We can go to the hospital right after the show. That's what Boone would want."

I stood there knowing Keith felt I should stay, not sure what my mother would think, not even sure what Boone would think. They expected me to win.

But I had won. It just all came clear, just like that, leaning against the back of a plush orchestra seat. I had won because I had something more important to do at this particular moment than sit down and wait for the winner to be announced. The timing was off, I shouldn't have had such a
202

choice to make, but the time was now. I needed to go to Boone.

"I'm going, Keith. You accept for me if I get it and congratulate the winner if I don't. And you don't even have to cry all the way home if I don't get it. I'll be at the hospital."

"I'll get a cab."

I hadn't thought of that.

The cab met us at the side entrance. Keith bent and gave me a glancing kiss on the cheek as the cab pulled away from the curb.

The taxi ride was a nightmare. I could not get any thoughts at all together in my head. It was as if I were holding my breath through the whole ride.

We pulled up in front of the hospital. "How much is it?" I asked.

"Your young man paid me already. Nice-looking dude."

"Thank you," I said. I tried to bring Keith into focus, but I could not. I walked up the steps to the hospital and raced to the elevator. I went up to Boone's floor, got off the elevator and went directly to his room. I just wanted to see him. I didn't want to speak to anyone else. I walked into the room I'd been visiting almost daily, and now it was not the same.

Boone made such a small difference in the white sheets on the hospital bed. He had a needle taped in his arm, and a tube ran through a strange machine that pulsed green and then up to a

203

plastic bag of clear fluid. Above his head and to the side another machine crouched, a rhythmic line tracing and vanishing across its screen in regular hills and valleys. He was connected to the machine by a tangle of wires. Another clear plastic tube was clipped somehow to his nose.

He was not unconscious. He looked up as I entered. "What are you doing here? The Emmys are on."

"I know. I'll catch a rerun. Wanted to see you. Just thought I'd drop by."

Boone turned on the TV set above his bed and the Emmys came into focus. He turned the sound down. "We'll listen when they get to something interesting, like you."

"Just think if we'd planned it this way," I said. "We could have done it with a flash to your room: 'Direct from St. John's with the great director Adam Michael Boone.' "

"You know, Kristin, I want to tell you something and I think this might be a good time. You're the only kid I ever could stand."

"Thanks," I said.

"You'll win. I actually saw your movie a few weeks ago. You're the best."

"I don't care, Boone," I said.

"That's good, Kristin. It'll only be true for a little while, but it's good."

Boone started to cough. He was in so much pain that I felt it streaming from him, filling up the room, the air, all of me as well as him.

"Oh, Boone, Boone."

I could see that despite the pain, he was there for me, his attention on me. Oh, how *much* love is.

"I wish you were my father, Boone. So much."

His face lost all sign of pain. It eased into a peaceful expression — one I'd never seen on his face before.

"Thank you," he said. "I wish I were too." He was crying, Boone was, and I felt joy at his words. But Boone could never resist a shot at a good line. "I think I'd give up any two of my Emmys for that to be true."

I laughed. I knew he wanted me to.

He coughed again. "Not true that last. I'd give them all up."

I knew that I probably shouldn't cross all the wires, but I did. I leaned over him and kissed him, first one cheek, then the other.

"The scene plays well," he said, and started to cough again.

The nurse came in and said, "You'll have to leave right now."

I waited outside the door of his room for the nurse to come out. "Please," I said to her. "Please tell me what's happening."

"Honey, I haven't got time to talk now. We're taking good care of him. You go wait in the waiting room and I'll come and talk to you when I have time."

The waiting room was empty, its seats around the room and some benches all waiting for someone to come into its isolation, to wait.

There was a TV on, its sound turned very low, in the corner of the room. Tuned to the Emmys. And I in my new blue gown watched while I waited.

I won.

I watched Keith accept my Emmy. "Kristin's sorry she couldn't be here," he said. "But this is better in a way, because I can say thank you just like she could, but I can also say that she really deserved it."

People laughed and applauded and the moment was over.

I waited.

The show was still going on when the nurse came, through the singing and dancing and acceptance speeches, to get me. I knew as soon as I saw her face that she hadn't come to take me to Boone's room.

"I'm sorry, dear," she said. "He had another embolism. It was more than he could handle."

"Boone's dead?" I whispered. But I didn't believe it. I would never believe it.

"He's dead," she said.

"What should I do?"

"Go down to the lobby. Your mother's waiting for you."

I just did what I was told.

My mother was in the lobby. I walked up to her. "He's dead," I told her.

"I know," she said. "I saw the doctor."

"How long have you been here?"

"When you weren't at the Emmys, I came here."

"You've been waiting outside this whole time?"

"Yes. I didn't want to come up and interrupt your time with Boone. I was worried. I just needed to be here." And she put her arms around me and held me to her.

"Mom, I told him I wish he'd been my father. He said he was glad I said that."

"Baby, I would have been very proud if he'd been your father."

She still held her arm around me as we walked toward the hospital exit.

"You won, you know."

"I saw it on the TV in the waiting room. It doesn't mean a thing."

"Later you'll feel good about it."

I couldn't get the sight of Boone back there in the bed out of my mind. I started crying.

She took out her handkerchief and dabbed at my eyes.

"You know, Kristin, when I watched him on Sonny Johnson's show that night, I found myself thinking that the three of us together would sure have a lot of fun. Boone knew that the trick is to keep laughing all the time you're not crying.''

My mother put it so well that it made it possible for me to get the image of him dying out of my mind and the image of him directing me back into my mind. Then I thought of our night at Swensen's.

My mother and I opened the hospital door and stepped into the cold air, hand in hand.

A flashbulb popped. Reporters were waiting. ''How do you feel about the Emmy?'' ''Is Boone dead?'' ''Are you sorry you left the awards?''

More and more flashbulbs and questions.

I was speechless. My mother wasn't. ''Get away from her, you vultures. There will be no comments tonight.''

They followed us to our car, still popping bulbs. I got in and slammed the door as quickly as I could. My mother went round to her side, got in and started up the motor. They were taking pictures to the last second, till she clearly showed she would run them down.

We drove off.

''Boone would have loved it, Mom, where you nearly threw that reporter a couple of hundred feet.''

''No reason to think he isn't taking notice, Kristin.''

I liked that idea.

If it's true, Boone, and if you're taking notice,

please stay with me a long, long time. I still need a lot of direction.

CODA

At the Academy Awards a special Oscar was given posthumously to Adam Michael Boone for his contributions to American film as both actor and director.

Probably because of that, the network reran the Sonny Johnson program that Boone and I had been on. I watched and cried. It had been less than a year ago, but I looked so much younger. Boone, of course, looked just like Boone.

ABOUT THE AUTHORS

Karen Rose was born in Brooklyn, New York, and currently lives in Los Angeles. She was an elementary school teacher for eighteen years and is now a full-time writer with five books to her credit. Lynda Halfyard, who was born in Grosse Pointe, Michigan, lives in Santa Monica. The idea for this book originated when they discovered their mutual interest in the actor Michael Dunn. Being both writers and movie buffs, they decided to collaborate on a novel with a built-in movie.